THE ACCIDENTAL MASTER

A PUPPY PLAY ROMANCE

M.A. INNES

1

JACKSON

"**M**elissa! What the hell did you put in that Facebook ad? I'm getting all kinds of crazy-ass responses!" Storming into the house, I slammed the door behind me. She was dead meat. She had to have pulled that shit on purpose.

What the hell had I done to her?

I headed for her bedroom, stomping up the stairs. Knowing my sister, she was probably buried up to her neck in books and papers. Normally, I wouldn't let myself into her house—I actually had manners unlike some people I could name—but this time, she'd gone too far. She wasn't going to be able to hide from me.

"Melissa!"

"What?" She was sitting on the bed surrounded by papers and notebooks, a half-eaten sandwich hanging off a plate. "What crawled up your ass and died?"

"What—" She wasn't serious? "I'll tell you what '*crawled up my ass*'—because it's your fault. I want to know what you did to my business. That ad you set up? The one you said was a simple Facebook ad that would help my business? What did you put in it?"

I tried to take a deep breath and slow down, but I was too angry and too confused. "I'm getting all kinds of crazy people calling me, and the emails are even worse. I had one from a guy in some weird European country I've never heard of, who wanted to know if I did training packages and not just individual sessions. He said he couldn't figure out from the site what kind of training I did with my pups. He wasn't talking about *dogs*!"

"Huh?" She seemed lost. "What do you mean he wasn't..."

Her voice trailed off, and she got a faraway look in her eyes before they widened, and her mouth opened. "*Ohhh...*"

"Do you know how long it took me to figure out he wasn't referring to beagles or boxers? Entirely too *fuckin'* long!" Just the fact that it'd taken almost five minutes before I finally understood what he was talking about had been the most embarrassing thing. I was a to-each-his-own kind of guy, but it was getting ridiculous.

"Oh, Jackie, I'm—"

I broke in. "Don't you '*Oh, Jackie*' me. I'm not six years old following you around like a lost puppy—ha! Puppy! What did you do?"

"Jackson, I'm so sorry. It was an accident—" If I hadn't known her so well, the innocent, crushed look would have worked.

"Like the *accident* where you dumped water on my pants at dinner? Or the *accident* where you put salt in my tea?"

"No, this was a *real* accident, and come on, I wouldn't do something like that to you. You know me."

Bullshit. "The salt incident was last month, and you dumped the water on me last week when you thought I was rude to the waiter."

"You *were* rude." She looked like she was still ready to take up the fight for the lazy waiter.

"That's not the point. *What did you do to my business?*" My voice was getting louder, but I couldn't control it. She'd talked me into trying some new marketing ideas, and now it looked like my business was falling down around me.

She slumped down onto the bed and gave me her best innocent look. If she'd pulled it on anyone else, they might have believed her. "I haven't fallen for that in years, so cut the crap."

Sighing, she slouched back against the pillows. "It *was* an accident. I promise. I was putting it together late the other night, and I must have mixed some things up. I'll go in and cancel the ad and get it corrected."

"Bullshit. You *accidentally* changed my dog training business to some kind of kink training center?" We might have tortured each other a bit over the years; it was what siblings did after all, but this crossed the line.

Dragging a pillow over her head, she moaned. This time her frustration sounded real. "I can't believe this."

"*You* can't believe it? What about *me*? I'm the one having to answer emails with naked pictures in them. Well, mostly naked. Several had tails!" They were insane and weird and a little too…no, I wasn't going down that rabbit hole right now.

I'd worry about my sanity and my new porn preferences another time. "*Just tails*, Melissa!"

And erections…

And teasing, happy smiles…

And I had to get back on track.

"I'm sorry! I'll fix it." She was still buried under the pillow, trying to pretend to be the injured party.

"How about I go into your work and say crazy shit about you? Let's see how you like that. You went too far with the crazy this time!"

"It wasn't on purpose!"

Yeah, she accidentally turned my dog training center into a BDSM business. At least, I thought it fell under BDSM.

Maybe not? "Bullshit! How can you even think I'd believe that line of crap?"

"Because it's true. I got the copy mixed up. I was putting up another ad at the same time!"

I was finally starting to connect the dots. Maybe. "What? What kind of ad were you posting?"

Had I stepped in something personal? Melissa had always been more private than I was about who she dated, but I didn't think she'd leave out something—who was I kidding? She would never have said anything. "Mellie, I won't tell Mom if that's what you're—"

"No, it's not for me. I'm not that interesting." She sighed again and looked up at the ceiling like she was praying for patience or for God to strike her dead. "I'm a writer. My newest book just came out, and I was putting together a Facebook ad that was designed to target specific people. I mixed them up. It was late, and I must have attached the wrong pictures."

She did what?

"You're a writer?" By the look on her face and the people who'd been emailing me, she didn't write historical romance. "You write dirty books? Does Mom know?"

"Of course she doesn't. No one in the family does. I really didn't mean to mess this up for you. I'll fix it right now. It's not hard to cancel the ad, and I'll do my best to help clean things up online. I'm sorry, Jackie."

"Stop it with the nicknames. You're just trying to manipulate me."

"Ja—"

"No. You're not going to distract me."

"I'm sorry, Jackson. Just don't say anything about the books. Please? I'm not ready to answer the questions." She finally looked like she wasn't trying to give me a line of shit.

"Yeah, there'd be questions, all right. Puppies? What do you write? Do I even want to know?" Probably not.

She huffed and gave me a stern look. "I write love stories that are a little unique."

"That's an understatement." At least, judging by the emails I was getting.

"Not helping, Jackson." She was starting to get her back up, and I could see that in her mind, she was building it up so that *she* was the injured party.

I shrugged. I wasn't trying to help; I was well past that. "I just want to know that you can fix this without damaging my business. And don't give me that look. I'm the one whose company is going to explode. Do you know what will happen if this gets out?"

Half of my clients were little old ladies and their uncontrollable yappy dogs. They wouldn't find it funny. Hell, I wasn't finding it funny. I'd been shocked when I first figured out what was going on, but after that, I'd been...confused. So confused, I'd spent several hours looking things up online before I'd come over to scream at her.

"I know." She sounded like a put-out teenager again.

"Just fix it. And no more advertising online." Everything was fine. I shouldn't have let her talk me into it to begin with. Training classes were always full, and I'd always found word-of-mouth referrals to be the best way to build up my business.

"But it's a great way—"

"No."

"Fine. But you're not going to tell Mom, right?"

"My telling Mom is the least of your worries. You should be thinking about how I'm going to get even with you!" My revenge was going to be good. It was just going to take some time to pick out exactly how to get her back.

"That's not fair! It was an accident."

"That's what you said about the salt *and* the water. I'm not falling for that bullshit again." I really should learn to watch my back around her better.

She got that innocent, sweet look again. "I'm your sister. That means you should trust me."

"Hell, no. I may love you, but most of the time, I don't believe a single word out of your mouth." The writing thing was starting to make sense.

I got a grin from her. "Aww, you say the sweetest things, Jackie. I love you too."

Deciding to ignore the nickname, I shook my head. "That's all you got out of that sentence?"

She gave me a smile that looked half-psychotic and half-sweet. My family was nuts. "I focused on the important part. Now, go away. I have work to do and an ad to take down."

"You really write dirty books? Like for a living?" I was still having a hard time wrapping my mind around it.

"Yup, and I'm doing pretty well." She smirked like she was very proud of herself. And probably glad she had someone to brag to now.

"Like *quit your day job* kind of good?" How much could you really make writing dirty books?

"None of your business." Then she gave me a teasing grin. "But possibly."

I shook my head and started for the door. I didn't want to know any more. If I wasn't careful, she would tell me exactly what she wrote just to make me crazy. "You're going to fix it right now? Like take the ads down and no more weird people emailing me?"

"I'll fix it."

"You'd better." I wasn't sure what I would do if it kept up. It was getting to be too much.

PULLING INTO MY DRIVEWAY, I THREW THE CAR INTO PARK and slouched back in the seat. *God, what a long day.* Maybe I

6

could have found more humor in the situation if it wasn't so confusing. I'd come out young, and while I wasn't a man-whore, I dated a lot and assumed I knew myself.

I was starting to suspect that I didn't understand myself as well as I'd thought.

Once I'd figured out what was going on, I'd checked my email and had seen about a dozen, all with the same theme. They might have said they were looking for training, but they'd just been guys in desperate need of attention and someone who understood. The emails had been from a variety of places. There had even been one older guy who, as he put it, "was finally ready to figure out who he was."

I'd replied as politely as I could. Partly because I was raised with manners and was representing my business—but a bigger part was because I felt bad. It was crazy, but I felt terrible that I couldn't help them. Completely nuts, but I hated telling them it was a mix-up.

The notification sound on my phone made me sit up and function. Swiping my finger across the screen, Melissa's text came up.

Sorry…ad taken down…shouldn't have any more calls.

Texting back a quick acknowledgment, I forced myself to get out of the car. Heading inside through the kitchen, I grabbed a beer out of the fridge and went to the living room. I had tons of budgeting and paperwork I should have been doing, but my brain wasn't going to cooperate so I walked back to my bedroom.

I could still see the pictures in my head every time I closed my eyes. And not just the ones that had been emailed to me. The videos and photos I'd seen online had been mind-blowing. I'd seen my fair share of porn, but I'd always gone more mainstream when I looked for something to watch.

I'd never even been curious enough to explore any of the fetish sites that were out there. Maybe I was boring, but I was pretty content with watching a blowjob scene or two guys going at it. The most adventurous thing I could remember looking at was a threesome video that had been pretty hot. But *nothing* like what I'd seen earlier.

It was so much more erotic than I'd expected.

There'd mostly been amateur stuff, but that made it even better. They were real people who found it arousing, not just actors getting paid. To say I was conflicted would've been an understatement.

Setting my beer down on the nightstand, I grabbed my laptop and took a deep breath. There couldn't be *that* many more emails, because the last of the phone calls had been before I'd gone over to Melissa's. Pulling up my account, I lay down on the bed and logged in.

There were only a few, and most of them were actual clients. In fact, there was only one that I didn't recognize, and the email address gave it away immediately: *twofunnypups*. Hating that I was going to have to burst someone else's fantasy, I clicked on it.

To Whom It May Concern:

We just wanted to thank you for training pups. So much of the BDSM community is focused on other things, and it's hard to find opportunities like this. My friend Cooper and I are pups. We've been friends for a long time and we have fun together, but we've always talked about taking things further. Training sounds interesting, but we have some questions.

First was if you would take pups to train together.

We don't do playtime apart. We're not exactly a traditional couple, but we've always been in this together, and I don't think I could do it without him. The second was if you helped single pups find an owner or master? Cooper and I have looked online, but it's hard because most masters want just one pup. Two seems kind of a handful. And I won't lie. We are. We try to be good, but things get out of hand. Cooper's easily excited and playful, and I don't know how I would describe me.

THE AD DIDN'T SAY HOW MUCH TRAINING COSTS, AND IT WAS kind of vague about if we would have to live there. I think we're close to you, so that might not be a problem, but we both have jobs that we can't afford to lose. We're not sure how it would work. So I guess we have lots of questions, not just a couple. But even if you can't train two pups like us, we wanted to say thanks. Seeing the ad made us feel good—like there were other people out there like us.

THANK YOU,
    Sawyer

MY HEART SANK.

It was sweet, and the picture they'd attached was just as cute. And thankfully, a lot more clothed than some of the other ones had been. They were sitting on a bench, arms slung around each other, grinning for the camera. They looked young but luckily not like jailbait.

I hit the reply button and looked at the email for a long time. It shouldn't have been hard. I'd written the reply so many times already; it felt like I could've done it in my sleep. Looking at the picture, though, I tried to guess who was Cooper and who was Sawyer.

They wanted to belong to the same master.

What did Sawyer mean when he said they weren't exactly a couple?

Telling myself it didn't matter and it wasn't my business, I took a drink of my beer before I set it down and started to type. It was going to be a long night. Knowing I needed to respond, no matter how hard it was going to be, I began.

DEAR SAWYER AND COOPER,

2

SAWYER

"Did he respond yet? Did you get an email from the Master?" Cooper's excited voice called out from the kitchen, and my stomach leaped into my throat.

We had.

But just the start of it made my heart sink. Not for me—I hadn't really thought it would work out anyway, but Cooper... he was going to be heartbroken. Oh, he might smile and tell me how it would happen next time, but I knew inside it would weigh on him.

Thank you for your interest, but...

Just the preview of the email screamed out that he didn't want us. Maybe he'd say something about other applicants or not accepting anyone else at that moment, but it would all boil down to the same thing—two pups were a lot of work.

I knew it was a big emotional commitment too. We'd done enough research to see how close a master and pup could be. It wasn't like we were going into the lifestyle blindly. Masters could picture getting to know one and training them but two... that meant drama and stress in most people's minds.

They didn't understand that Cooper and I weren't like that.

Maybe if we'd started this when we first got out of high school, it would have been different, but now we were a family. How could I be jealous of their relationship when I'd have one with him too? We were so different, it wouldn't be the same thing.

Cooper would want to have Master throw the ball for him or play, and I wanted someone to curl up with. Someone to cuddle who would pet me and—

"Have you checked yet?" Cooper's head popped out around the doorframe. "Sawyer?"

"What?" It took me a second to process what he was saying. "The email?"

Internally, I sighed. I didn't want to tell him that we'd gotten the reply. I wanted to protect him from whatever rejection was in the email, but I knew it wouldn't work. We'd made a vow when I'd first found out about the puppy stuff that we weren't going to lie to each other. Family didn't lie.

At least, our family didn't.

"Yes!" He grinned, shaking his head at me. "Dinner's almost ready. Did you check?"

Cooper glanced down at the laptop in my hands, and I could see him barely holding back a little happy dance. We'd saved for months for the computer, and finally being able to walk into the store and buy it made him so excited it was like watching a football player do a touchdown dance.

Except my excited guy was a lean little twink, not a big hulking athlete.

"Yes, I haven't opened it yet, though." And I didn't want to, but Cooper already knew that.

"It doesn't matter if we can't do it. Maybe it's too expensive, or he's already full. We tried, and we started planning the next step. That's what matters. It's like going out for job interviews. You keep trying until you find the right company." Cooper had endless faith that things would work out.

When we were living in the rent-by-the-week roach motel, I was counting down the hours until we were living on the street, but he was always so positive it made me crazy some days. Now I counted on it and held it close. Things had finally started turning around for us, and I wanted to believe they could just keep getting better.

It was hard to believe.

Cooper bounced across the room. He didn't see it, but it was like his puppy persona was so close to the surface it would leak out when he was doing everyday stuff. I thought it was why he was so popular at the coffee shop where he worked. People loved the innocent excitement that radiated from him.

"Let me see." He grinned and curled up next to me on the couch, wrapping his body around mine.

Once we'd crossed the line from friendship to more, he went from having a small bubble of personal space near me to none at all. It was like once he knew it was okay, he held nothing back. I leaned into him and turned the laptop so he could see.

"Oh. That doesn't sound good." He sighed. "But maybe he'll know a master who's looking for pups."

"Maybe." Clicking on the email, I mentally prepared myself for what was coming.

DEAR SAWYER AND COOPER,

Thank you for your interest, but there was a mix up between my business and another separate ad that was not related to my company. I run a traditional dog training center, not one that caters to alternative lifestyles. I am very sorry about the problem. It was not intended to be advertised that way, and the incorrect ad has been taken down.

This is usually where I've been stopping these emails, but I just wanted to say that your letter was very sincere. I know that if the right person had seen your email, they would have been interested in getting to know you both. You look like a cute couple, and I'm sure you'll find what you're looking for. This whole experience has made me think, and I want to thank you for that.

SINCERELY,
    Jackson Kent
    Riverwood Training Center

WELL, I WASN'T EXPECTING THAT.

"He's a real dog trainer?" Cooper blinked at me and turned to read the email again. "Like real dogs?"

"Evidently." Part of me wanted to laugh. Maybe it wasn't the right response, but knowing that he wasn't rejecting us because of anything personal was a relief. We weren't dogs. We liked to pretend we were puppies, but no amount of pretending would magically change that.

Cooper clearly wasn't sure what to think. He kept glancing back and forth between the screen and me. "I wasn't expecting that."

"Me neither." The initial Facebook ad had come up in some groups we belonged to, and it had been worded a little weirdly, but it'd looked interesting, so we'd thought we'd try.

"I guess we need to do more research next time." Cooper was still frustrated, but his growing smile showed that his normal cheer was starting to push its way to the surface. "He must have been shocked. It sounds like we weren't the only people who contacted him. Can you imagine how horrified he probably was?"

Copper giggled and relaxed his head on my shoulder. "He was very polite, though."

"He has a real business, so he doesn't want to look bad."

The last thing the guy wanted was angry, kinky people raising hell online.

Shaking his head, Cooper pointed to the screen. "It's more than that. He said we're a cute couple and that someone else would've loved to have met us."

Okay, so that was more than a polite rejection. "We *are* cute." Cooper laughed, so I kept going. "Maybe we're so cute we turned him gay."

Giggling, Cooper nodded. "Maybe we've turned him gay and made him curious about being a master?"

I had to smile. "We probably turned him gay, but he's going to be a pup too."

Cooper groaned and turned his face into my neck. "Now you've jinxed us. I'm going to blame it on you if he turns out to be another new pup too."

I set the computer on the couch beside me and pulled Cooper into my arms. He sighed and cuddled deeper into me. Just by the way he moved, I knew he was closing his eyes and relaxing. He could fall asleep almost anywhere once he stopped moving.

It still amazed me that after everything he'd been through, he was still so sweet. He didn't let things make him bitter or angry. He just accepted problems and truly knew that they would get better. Wrapping my arms around him, I thought back to the first time I met him.

The first day of high school was overwhelming and frustrating. It was a huge building that pulled from a couple of different middle schools, so it was a sea of people, and I couldn't find anyone that I knew.

Not that I'd had many friends.

I knew I was gay early, and I also knew what people in my neighborhood would have thought, so I kept most of the other kids at a distance. Space kept me from worrying about people finding out, but as I pushed my way through the crowds, what I wanted more than anything was one familiar face.

What I found was Cooper.

He'd been a skinny little thing that hadn't gotten a growth spurt yet and looked like an easy target for the bullies. Something about him just screamed out that he wasn't as "macho" as the other guys. Nothing made it obvious he was gay, but I knew by looking at him.

The first time I saw him, there were a handful of bigger guys watching, clearly getting ready to pounce. Cooper had no idea what to do and was staring as they got closer. They were probably going to give him a good scare, but he was like some kind of frightened rabbit. I couldn't stand there and watch it happen.

Walking up behind him, I grabbed his shoulder and gave it a squeeze. "You didn't wait for me, Cooper. Come on, we're going to be late."

Giving the guys a long stare, I steered him down the hall. I wasn't that tall, but I was stocky and had grown up on the wrong side of town. I knew how to make it obvious I wouldn't put up with shit. Not from them at least. I'd seen scarier. These guys were just jocks with too much time on their hands and too little brains.

Once we'd made it around the corner, I'd stopped and tried to give him a reassuring smile. "You okay?"

It didn't seem to work.

He frowned at me and shrugged before charging in with his questions. "How did you know my name? Did we go to school together last year? Did you see how tall those guys were? What do you think they were doing to do? Do you think I'd really fit in a locker? Some guy said that when I first walked in."

I remember thinking he was like a bouncy chipmunk, but looking back, a yappy puppy would have been a better description. "Your name is on your backpack."

He stopped. "Oh."

I wasn't sure if his parents were trying to make him a target of every bully out there or if they were just that stupid. I should have walked away, but something about the expression on his face and how he made me feel pulled at me.

From that point on, we'd been inseparable.

The feel of his breath on my neck pulled me out of the memories. "Hey, if you go to sleep now, you're going to be up too early tomorrow."

"But…"

"Oh no. I'm not finding you flicking channels at three o'clock in the morning again."

"That was a long time ago." His relaxed voice made me want to curl up in bed with him. We'd both had long days.

"It was last week. I found you watching infomercials on cooking gadgets."

"Oh, that's right." He groaned as he sat up blinking at me with half-lidded eyes.

"And you haven't eaten dinner yet."

He smiled, and it looked sweet and sleepy. "I made dinner. It's done. That's what I came out to tell you."

"It smells great." The list of things we could cook was pretty basic, but neither of us had any lessons when we were younger. And for a long time, we'd barely had money for mac and cheese. But we were getting better.

"It's spaghetti, but this time I put sausage in the sauce and made garlic bread." He grinned. "It's not even burned."

That was better than last time then.

"I'm sure you did a great job." Standing, I grabbed his hand and pulled him up with me. "Let's go eat. I'm starved."

"Did you guys work through lunch again? I think you had an easier schedule when you were still out in the field."

He was probably right. But my job now paid a hell of a lot better. "We're just behind on the project. The client keeps changing their mind about how the garden needs to look. We've gone from formal and low maintenance to casual with an overgrown feel, and now they want us to look at making it 'sustainable' and listed off all kinds of environmental buzz words they don't know anything about. We told them we only used native plants and that we were conscious of how we planted things. Joshua is going in tomorrow to have a sit-down with them and show them another set of plans."

I might have started out mowing lawns and digging holes for ugly bushes, but it wasn't long before my hard work was noticed. Within six months of going to work full-time for the landscaping company, I'd caught the attention of one of the office guys who actually put the plans together for the bigger jobs. Another couple of months had me out of the yards and into the office.

It had been long months of sleepless nights and worries that I wasn't going to be able to take care of us, but once we hit that point, everything turned around.

Cooper frowned as he started walking with me toward the kitchen. "You need to make sure they realize how many hours you're working in a row. You didn't get lunch a couple of days this week. At least take a sandwich or something just in case they do it again."

He worried about me and it was so cute, but even after four years, I'd never gotten used to it. Living with my dad growing up meant I learned to get by on my own pretty fast. No one had ever followed behind me and made sure I'd eaten lunch or gotten enough sleep. Accepting it, and understanding it was his way of telling me he was thinking about me, had been one of the hardest things to realize when we'd first started living together.

"You're right. I need to keep some snacks in my desk too. At least until things calm down." Spring and summer were our busiest times of the year, and I was waiting for fall when things would start to relax. "Will you put that on the list, so we can remember to grab a few things at the store this weekend?"

Having enough money to randomly add stuff to the grocery list was still pretty new.

Cooper nodded, then frowned at the stove. "We need to work on that tomorrow. I want to see if we can come up with some different things to cook."

"Are you getting tired of spaghetti?"

He sighed. "Yeah. It was fine when that was all we could afford, but now we've got a real food budget, and I want to find some other stuff to make."

If he wanted us to figure out how to cook, that was what we would do. "How about we look for some recipes online later and find a few to try out?"

Cooper stepped close and wrapped his arms around me. "Thank you." Giving me a kiss, he pulled back and smiled. "I think it's going to work out."

"Dinner?"

"No." He laughed. "Finding a master and…just everything. We've both got good jobs and a savings account now, and this is the next step. I just know it."

Giving him a kiss on his forehead, I smiled. "We'll figure it out. Now, are you going to feed me or not?"

I might not have been as convinced it would be perfect as Cooper was, but I wasn't going to burst his bubble. His never-questioning faith that our life would work out kept us going through some rough times, and I wouldn't forget that.

3

―――――――

COOPER

Throwing myself down on a rickety folding chair wasn't much of a break, but it got me off my feet, so I wouldn't complain. I was entitled to twenty minutes, but all I wanted was five to check my email....Well, our email.

We each had regular email accounts, but we'd set up a separate one just for our puppy-play stuff. Keeping things private was a goal. Neither one of us wanted to be fired for something that was just our business to begin with. My company might not care, but I wasn't sure about Sawyer's, and he'd lose his mind if he got fired, so...low-key it was.

I'd been...naughty.

It wasn't terrible, and I didn't need to apologize to anyone, but I'd known what Sawyer would say if I asked him about it... so I hadn't asked. I was going to fess up—once I'd given Jackson a chance to answer back.

Sawyer was probably right. The trainer was probably gay— the cute comment and all—but he'd made it clear he wasn't looking for pups. At least not the naked, human kind. But something about the way he'd worded the letter, and how I felt as I'd read it, said there was something more to him.

Why even say we were cute or that we seemed sincere? And then there had been that last line about the experience making him think. I still wasn't sure how the ad could have gotten that mixed up, but he'd seemed very genuine. And when Sawyer had looked up the business later, he'd seen it was a real dog training center with nice facilities.

Not pissing off people who could bad-mouth you online and draw lots of attention to you was one thing, but he hadn't just been polite....There was more to it than that. Sawyer wanted to move on and give ourselves time to find other options. That didn't feel right, though.

So I'd emailed him back.

Sawyer was going to lose his marbles, but I had to.

I could hear the lecture already. He was going to say I was impulsive and that I'd make the guy uncomfortable or angry or that I was oversharing with strangers. He worried. He might end up being right. I knew that. But walking away felt wrong.

Pulling up the email account, I didn't see any responses to the note I'd sent last night, so I went back to reread my letter. Was it too much? Maybe. Had I overshared? Oh, yes. But that was the only way a lifestyle like this worked...with trust. If we weren't open, then it wouldn't work.

DEAR JACKSON,

Thank you for your letter and letting us know about the mix-up. Not hearing back would have been terrible, so I'm glad we heard from you even though it's frustrating. Not that I'm frustrated at you. Just the situation. I know Sawyer told you in our first letter that we're both pups and are looking to find a master. It's hard finding a man who's interested in not only a unique lifestyle but two guys who want a relationship with a third, but Sawyer and I are a package deal.

I know it's not the same thing, but you talk to people all

day long about the responsibility of owning a pet, and it's not that different, so I was wondering if you had any ideas about how to explain that having two pups isn't that much harder than one. I was just curious because you deal with dogs and people all day long. Again, thank you for answering our email.

Cooper

P.S. Thanks for saying we were cute.

So maybe it was a little rambly and awkward, but I hadn't been sure what to say. The only guy I'd ever kissed or did anything with was Sawyer, and flirting hadn't been something I was willing to even attempt in high school. I wasn't exactly in the closet, but my parents had very firm beliefs about behavior, and I wasn't willing to push their patience. I'd always figured I'd have time to learn about flirting and guys in college.

Well, things hadn't worked out the way I'd planned, but I wouldn't trade Sawyer for anything.

Still, no matter how much I loved Sawyer, I didn't have a really good idea about how to talk to a guy in this situation. Work, I was fine. Friends, I was pretty good. I even talked to the neighbors in our building without sounding like a moron. But trying to see if someone was interested...I wasn't sure I could do it.

Sawyer had more experience with men—I knew he could flirt when he wanted to. He was cautious about talking to people about the puppy stuff; it'd taken months to get him to agree to set up a separate Facebook account under a fake profile, so we could look for other pups and masters online.

Talking to Jackson was going to be up to me, at least to begin with. Sawyer had only written the first email because he'd known I was going to and wanted to protect me. He'd also try to protect me by talking me into moving on from Jackson, but something about that email just pulled at me.

Putting my phone away, I leaned back and stretched my legs. I rested my head against the wall and closed my eyes, enjoying the quiet. I loved my job, but some days it was insane. I'd been running nonstop since I'd come in midmorning, and I knew it wasn't going to slow down anytime soon.

Looking around the cramped room filled with boxes of cups and packages of coffee, I knew I was lucky. I'd found a job that I was going to grow into a career and worked with people who were open-minded and loving. I knew things could have gone very differently.

My parents had never been the most demonstrative people, but they'd taken care of me, and I'd thought everything was fine. All through high school, they'd talked about the skills I would need for college and how my future would look. Perfectly normal conversations. They'd even helped me apply to several universities.

But everything changed after graduation. I wasn't even eighteen. I'd woken up the next morning to hostile parents who wanted me out. They'd found out that not only was I gay but that I was into *foul* things, and they'd had enough. Being gay was something they couldn't kick me out for, but finding weird porn on my computer evidently was.

I don't know where I would have ended up if Sawyer hadn't been there.

He'd been my friend since the first day of high school, and he'd always watched out for me. Even when I was clueless. It'd taken me *too* long to figure out he was gay too. Just thinking about it made me smile. It'd been an awkward conversation where he'd needed to explain far too much and had helped me to understand we were both bottoms.

From then on, he was more like a brother than a friend. He was the person I could talk to about almost everything. When I

23

started packing things up to leave, he was the only one I called. He talked me through what to take and then met me outside the house.

Knowing I wasn't alone made walking away easier.

And knowing I still wasn't alone made reaching out to Jackson easier.

I wasn't naïve enough to think that everything would work out. Life wasn't a fairy tale. But sometimes you had to take a chance. And mostly, I was taking the chance for Sawyer. He was always trying to be strong for me and to do his best to take care of me, so I worried sometimes I wasn't doing enough to care for him.

That was why we needed a master. Not quite a Dom, because although spankings were fun, we weren't looking for something that intense. We needed someone to let us both relax and really sink into our puppy roles without feeling like something was missing. The occasional spanking was going to be a good bonus too.

Taking turns being the master or just being puppies together was fun, but it wasn't the full experience we both knew it could be. It had taken a while for Sawyer to get used to the possibility of having a master. What neither of us had realized was that finding someone who wanted us both would be hard.

"Who would have thought finding someone who wanted a long-term threesome with two hot guys would be hard?"

Not me.

April's head popped through the door, the rainbow of colors in her hair that week startling as they burst through the opening. "Hey, I know you're still on your break, but—"

I had to smile. She looked worried, but I'd known as soon as I'd snuck away I wasn't going to get much time. "It's fine. Today's crazy."

"But you've only—"

I jumped in again. "Don't worry about it. I promise. I'll take a longer break later in the day to make up for it."

April smiled, clearly relieved. She was a worrier. Some people probably wouldn't think so, but it made her a great manager. She never drove anyone crazy, and she always let people know how important they were. It made the turnover of staff so low at the coffee shop that it was a miracle they had an opening when I first applied.

My longer break didn't happen for hours—well past lunch, but I didn't mind. April kept worrying. "You haven't even eaten. What were you saying about Sawyer?"

She gave me a small smile when I frowned at her teasingly. "It's not the same thing. He's in an office and just doesn't want to point out to his obsessive boss that they need to pause and get food once in a while. We, on the other hand, haven't stopped moving. *See?* Not the same thing."

April giggled and finished wiping up the counters. "Well, unless you finally take that break, I might just happen to mention how much work you've been doing to that sexy man of yours the next time I come over for dinner."

"That's cheating." But smiling, I stopped restocking the shelves and went to the back, grateful to be able to relax. I only had another hour before I went home, and any rest I could get would be appreciated.

April smirked and followed me back to the storeroom. She hadn't taken any time off either, and now that some of the afternoon and evening staff had started to arrive, it was easier for her to step away. "That's what they teach in manager's school."

"I'm starting to think you've been making some of that up. The 'manager's school' classes I've been seeing don't list stuff like that." My online classes were going to be filled with practical things, not stupid one-liners that would be needed as a boss.

"How is registration going?" She closed the door and went over to sit in another one of the folding chairs.

"It's going good. I start my first class next month." I'd thought about it for a while, but I finally broke down a couple of months ago and started talking to Sawyer about taking online college courses.

We'd gone back and forth about what I should go to school for, and eventually, I'd agreed to go the whole way and get a full bachelor's degree. It was going to take a lot longer than four years, but I'd get it eventually. Without my parents' income to screw things up, I actually qualified for a lot of help financially, and it wasn't going to be the burden I'd initially thought it would.

"That's great!" April beamed. "You know, that might give you the leg up you need to be considered for the new management position that's going to open up, once they settle on the location of the next store."

I sighed. "Maybe, but it takes them so long to make a decision. That could be a year or two from now. And by that time, one of the other stores might have a better candidate."

She shrugged. "I don't think so. From what I've heard, everyone else is pretty settled and not looking to change things up. You're the only one who wants to leave."

I knew she was teasing, but I didn't like the way it sounded. "I don't want to leave you. It's just that—"

She reached over and gave my leg a pat, making her rainbow hair move like a living waterfall of color. Super distracting. "I know that, and it would be a great opportunity for you. You're good with the customers, and you have a great grasp on the paperwork and business side of things. Once the owners see that you're serious about furthering your education, it would only make sense for you to step into that role."

"I just hope they don't think it will magically happen overnight. I can really only manage one class at a time with the way they do things, or it will just be too much." I was starting to worry. What if going to school messed everything up? Sawyer never wanted to go, but he had always been my biggest supporter.

What if it changed things between us?

What if I didn't have enough time to do everything?

"I'm sure they would get that." She gave me an understanding smile. "It just feels like a lot, but you can do it. You're smart enough that I don't think it's going to be as difficult as you're imagining."

We'd had the same discussion multiple times over the previous weeks, and I kept telling myself she was right, but it was hard. I'd been so confident when I was getting ready for college the first time, and I wasn't sure where all of it had fled to.

I just needed to find it again.

"And I remembered what Sawyer said about how smart you are, and how good you did in high school. He brags about that every time the topic of school and future plans comes up." April shook her head, and her smile turned sweet. She thought Sawyer and I were the perfect couple. I always wondered what she would think if I told her about the role-playing stuff or the fact that we wanted a third in our relationship.

April was the most open-minded person I'd ever met; she'd probably understand. I just wasn't willing to take the chance. And Sawyer agreed with me. As hard as everything had been the first year, neither of us wanted to do anything that would rock the boat and potentially get us fired.

"He's sweet. But what he leaves out is how great he did too." I leaned back and smiled. "He did awesome when he put his mind to it."

Sawyer hadn't really cared. He had a handful of classes that he'd done wonderfully in, but for the most part, once a teacher pissed him off, he was done and just tuned out. He'd basically seen high school as a babysitter to keep kids occupied until they could go to college or enter the real world. And he'd been itching to hit the real world as soon as possible.

April nodded. "He comes across as smart."

"He's also good at giving guilt trips, so no tattling on me about the lack of breaks thing." It normally wasn't that hectic, but some kind of virus was going around, and we were short-staffed. I was thankful I hadn't gotten it, but I was really starting to think about taking a few days off once everyone was back at work.

She made an X over her heart and giggled. "I won't tell. I need you here until everyone is back on their feet. And not unexpectedly coming down with something because I pissed you off."

Laughing, I reached into my pocket to grab my phone. "No chance of that. The extra hours are going to look nice on my paycheck." Overtime was going to make sure we had enough money in our savings account to do something fun. I hadn't gotten Sawyer completely talked into it, but I was getting close. He'd never had a real vacation, and I wanted to do something special with him. I just had to figure out an option that was perfect and cheap.

"Mine too, but the big bosses are going to start to grumble if we don't get back up to fully staffed soon. They don't like seeing everyone being overworked. Tired, frustrated employees do not give the best customer service." April yawned and leaned her head back against the wall.

Swiping my finger across the screen, I sent a quick message to Sawyer reminding him that I was going to be home later than usual and checked my email. Nothing yet. I wasn't sure if that was a good thing or not.

Jackson might have been working and not had the time to check his emails, but he also might be staring at the screen trying to figure out how to politely tell the weird guy how to back off. It would have been easier to leave it alone if he hadn't been so nice and if he hadn't been so cute.

There were only a handful of pictures that seemed like they were him on the website, but something about the way he looked at the camera and the dogs he was training screamed out that he was more dominant than he admitted. Maybe he just hadn't realized it. His letter had said something about the whole experience making him think.

I hoped he was thinking about us.

4

JACKSON

Staring at the computer wasn't helping me figure out how to answer Cooper. He was so earnest and sweet that I couldn't ignore it. It was also impossible to tell him I couldn't help or to chase him away.

I wasn't sure what I wanted, but I knew scaring him off wasn't it.

Sawyer had sounded so polite and composed, but Cooper's letter came across as excited and needy. Not in a negative way, but it made me want to pull him into my arms and tell him we'd work everything out.

Hell if I knew what that would look like.

I was picturing him as an excited pup who'd run and need lots of exercise. Which was cute, except that he wasn't a real pup—and that he'd be naked or nearly naked while crawling around.

I might be wrong about that part; from what I'd seen online, there was a range of...costumes...outfits...that the pups wore. But in the pictures I'd been sent, most of them weren't wearing that many clothes. Tails, gloves, masks, ears, collars...just not pants.

Except the one guy who hadn't spoken much English and who'd seemed to be wearing a full poodle costume.

It'd been interesting, and the gentleman was polite, but something about Sawyer and Cooper just kept me coming back to them. I wasn't sure what made them different, but where I could ignore the other emails and respond to them politely and professionally, something about theirs was making walking away a struggle.

I'd tried.

I'd seen his email at lunch when I'd finally taken a break from paperwork and training classes, and it had been the only thing I could think about all afternoon. I was supposed to be headed to bed after an incredibly long day, but I hadn't even eaten dinner yet, much less figured out how to respond. And I'd lost track of the number of beers I'd had while I'd stared at the email. The practical side of me said to ignore it and walk away, but I couldn't.

Was he flirting? It almost sounded that way. But they were younger and clearly looking for things I'd never considered.

A master.

A three-way relationship.

Someone who could accept that they were pups at heart.

I wasn't the most traditionally dominant guy with people. I liked my space and doing my own thing. But I could see how some of the ways I interacted with dogs might apply in the kind of relationship they were talking about. If what I was seeing online was accurate.

That was still up in the air.

Some sites seemed informative and practical—as if they were doing tutorials on how to unclog the drain or building some project at home. Others had fantasies and porn, probably not real at all. But there were sites and blogs that I couldn't put in one category or another.

They felt real, but I couldn't picture myself in the situations, so it was impossible to tell.

Looking around the living room, the wide-open space would be perfect for animals. But human pups? Could I picture one of them curled up in front of the fireplace on a dog bed just for them while the other was curled up beside me on the couch?

Possibly.

I wasn't sure I could see throwing a ball for a guy dressed up as a puppy. But I also wasn't ready to let them go, because after hours of looking at the computer, and a few too many beers, I was hitting the little back arrow to respond.

But how did I start? What was I supposed to say? Cooper was clearly reaching out, but to what end?

Finally, I stopped worrying and started. It was probably beer-induced confidence.

DEAR COOPER,

Having two dogs is hard, but when you love them both, it makes the difficult parts easier to work through. I would have to think it would be the same with two men, puppy play or not. I think being honest with whoever you are interested in is the biggest thing.

Maybe you should look for guys (and I apologize if I say any of this wrong) who have been masters in the past but who haven't participated in it lately. Or possibly even guys who are new to the scene. You might find that they are more curious than they would expect when they start getting more information.

Just be prepared for a lot of questions from new people. I don't know how long you both have been exploring puppy play, but from what I've seen online, it's a little confusing. But it sounds like you both know what you're looking for out of a relationship. Am I right in assuming that a master would be like a third person in your relationship? I think it's great that you're so confident about what you want. Being open with people is probably hard, but I appreciate how honest you've both been with me.

Jackson

BEFORE I COULD QUESTION MY DECISION TO RESPOND, MUCH less what I'd written, I hit send. It felt like the email had been full of mixed messages, but I wasn't sure what I was trying to hint at. Just reading Cooper's email was thought-provoking, and it had all kinds of questions running through my head.

Were they looking for a third?

What did a master do with pups?

What kind of pups were they?

I had more questions than anything, and even if we continued to email back and forth, I wasn't sure if I'd be able to get all of them answered. If all I did was throw out questions, it would probably feel like an interrogation and not a friendly discussion.

Was that what I was aiming for? Friends?

When the phone started ringing, I knew I shouldn't answer it. But Melissa hated being ignored, and I wasn't sure it was worth the consequence of letting it go to voicemail. Picking the phone up off the couch beside me, I swiped my finger across the screen. "Mellie, I don't want to argue with you."

She laughed. "How much have you had to drink, lightweight?"

"Don't call me that. And I don't know." I had more tolerance than I used to. And I wasn't drunk. Just relaxed.

"Jackie, you're the biggest lightweight I know."

I sighed, a clear sign I was more intoxicated than I realized —not that I was going to pay attention to it. "It's all your fault."

"That you can't hold your alcohol?" I could hear her snicker.

"No, for getting me into this mess to begin with. I was very happy being very vanilla. I didn't even realize I was vanilla I was that vanilla." Had that sentence made sense? It had in my head, but I was exhausted, and my mind had been running in circles for hours.

"That didn't make as much sense as you thought it did, Jackie."

Damn.

"You can't tell Mom." It sounded like we were kids again, but I wasn't ready to have this conversation with anyone else. Not yet. Probably not ever. Maybe.

She sounded offended. "I didn't tell her about randy Randy, did I?"

Oh, I hadn't thought about him in a long time. "No, you were a good sister."

"So, spill." She tried to sound bored, but I could hear the curiosity in her voice.

"Well, you know the whole mix-up thing with the ad?"

She sighed, clearly starting to get frustrated. "I already apologized for that—"

"No, no, no, I'm not mad. I emailed everyone back and got it cleared up, but I started talking to some guys and now..." I wasn't sure what to say because I wasn't really sure what I was doing with Cooper and Sawyer.

"How many of these guys are you talking to?" Now I had her attention. That was probably a bad thing.

But the way she'd said it made it sound like I was collecting a harem of pups. "They're a couple. Not *lots* of guys."

"You're talking with a master and his pup?" She sounded confused. It wasn't that hard to follow. She just wasn't paying attention. "Jackie, does being a pup sound appealing?"

"No. And stop calling me that." She really wasn't listening. "Cooper and Sawyer are both pups."

"*Both* pups?"

Why was I having to repeat everything? "Yes, I just said that."

Hadn't I?

She snorted. "Then try again with more words this time, genius."

I was going to have to break it all down for her. She clearly wasn't following. "They emailed me. They're a couple and are *both* the pup. They're looking for a master. They thought I could help them find one."

"Ohhh." She dragged the word out like she was finally connecting the dots. "And you've been talking to the guys?"

"Just a few emails back and forth." A few confusing letters that sucked me in. Like a black hole. Like the tub drain. And no more beer for me. I leaned over and pushed the bottle on the coffee table farther from me. "They're looking for a master for both of them."

She was silent for a moment. "And what do you think about that?"

I said the first thing that popped into my head. "I think they're cute."

Another short silence. "How do you know they're cute?"

I couldn't tell if it was laughter in her voice or if it was curiosity. Either way, the question was stupid. "They sent a picture."

"What kind of picture?" Now the laughter was clear.

I snorted. "Not *that* kind. They're fully dressed."

She chuckled again. "Good to know. Do you like talking to them?"

"Writing to them." I shouldn't have to keep correcting her. "Yes."

"Writing, sorry. What do you think about them being pups?"

"No idea." That was kind of the reason I brought it up, *duh*. "I've been looking it up online."

"Have you talked to them about what they're looking for in a master?" She was trying to treat it very matter-of-factly, which I appreciated.

"No."

"That might be helpful then." I could hear the *duhhh* in her voice.

"Maybe." I wasn't ready to commit to that yet.

She mumbled something about *maybe, my ass*, but I ignored that part. "It's just been a few emails."

"From the people I've talked to and the research I've done, everyone in the scene does it differently, but mostly it's about a different way of showing affection and love. The submissive partner gets to cuddle and play without all the worries that come with being an adult." There was a pause before she continued. "I think you need to look at your past relationships and see what parts were the most important to you, and then see how those pieces relate to the lifestyle. And ask them questions."

"Maybe."

"And *maybe* I won't drive you crazy about the fact that it's two submissives you're currently obsessing over."

"I'm not obsessing." I was not going to agree to that.

"You are. Remember the UPS guy?"

"That's not important." Bringing up the UPS guy was a low blow, even for her.

"I'll drop it if you actually ask them questions."

"All right." That wasn't hard to promise.

"Real questions? Not like *how's the weather* bullshit."

"That's something you'd pull, *Ms. My Final Exam Essays Almost Got Me Kicked Out of School*."

She laughed. "Don't email again until you're sober."

"I'm not drunk. Just relaxed."

"So relaxed you told your sister that you were interested in getting to know two *cute* guys who both wear tails—I'm assuming they have tails—and want a master to care for them?"

Shit.

"Don't tell Mom, or I'll tell her you write dirty books." That was going to be my go-to threat for years. I loved it.

"You said you wouldn't tell."

She knew better than to believe that. "You keep my secret, and I'll keep yours."

Melissa gave a short hum that could have meant acceptance or that she was planning on taking over the world. "You know, if you keep them, she's going to find out, eventually."

"If I throw you under the bus first, then she won't care as much." That idea was starting to sound perfect. "Her pretty, sweet baby girl lying to her will be more important than my dating two men."

"Dating, huh?"

"Shut up." I had to get off the phone before I told her how much I'd been researching online. "I'm going to bed."

I could hear her trying to cover up her laughter. "Have fun."

That sounded dirty. "I will *not*. Go away."

She was still laughing as I ended the call.

She'd actually given me some good advice, but I wasn't sure of the best way to start. Was I supposed to email him again? Wait until my questions came up naturally in the conversation? What if he thought my lack of questions meant I wasn't interested? What if he thought I asked too many questions? What if he didn't email back?

Listing off all the what-if's and problems that were running through my head was too much. So I tried to focus on the things I did know.

I was a damned good dog trainer. I knew how to soothe

dogs that were frightened and take control of dogs desperately in need of a leader in their pack. I read people fairly well. I wasn't afraid of a challenge or hard work. I'd started my own business, after all. And I was damn good in bed. Even my exes who'd said I was a bit controlling and had a tendency to hover had no complaints about my prowess in the bedroom, or the kitchen, or the living room. Or even that time at the movies.

Hmm. Maybe I wasn't as vanilla as I'd thought.

But could I see myself with two men? That was probably the best place to start. Kinks and preferences aside, could I see having a relationship with not one younger guy, but two? Did their ages even matter? I'd dated a bit younger and slightly older, but I was usually more focused on the person than anything else, so I didn't think so.

But how would three people change the dynamic in a relationship? Would I be a third wheel?

Would they even want someone who was older? I wasn't ancient by any definition, but I wasn't in my twenties any longer, and that might make a difference to them. I wasn't bad-looking; I knew that. But forty was a long way from the young guys I'd seen in the picture.

I'd thought it might be fake for a moment when I'd first seen it, but I quickly dismissed that. They honestly thought they were applying to be part of a training program, so there was no way scamming me out of anything could have been their game. No, they really were that sweet. I could feel it deep inside every time I looked at the image and read the emails.

I was tired and hungry, but the questions were eating at me. Opening my computer again, I pulled up the search engine and tried to think of what to research first. I'd start at the beginning. There were layers of things I didn't understand, but there was one basic issue that had to be ironed out first.

Can a relationship with three people work?

5

SAWYER

"Sawyer? I have to—"

"Cooper what did you—"

We'd both spoken at the same time as Cooper had come blasting in the front door, but now that he was standing in front of me, he was quiet and looking anywhere but at me. "Coop, what did you do?"

I held up my phone, which was opened to the mail app, and stared at him. He sighed, finally meeting my eyes. "I was going to tell you. I hoped I'd get home before you even thought to look. You don't check that email account very often unless you're expecting something."

Lying would make us both feel worse, so I shrugged, trying not to blush, and opened my arms to Cooper. "I wanted to read the emails again."

He stepped into me and sighed, curling his body as close to mine as he could. "I emailed him back. I couldn't help it."

I'd thought about doing the same thing, so I couldn't say much. "He's not even in the lifestyle, Coop."

"But he seemed curious in the email. That's how everything new starts. You see something and then it won't leave your head, so you have to look into it more." Cooper gave my cheek a kiss and leaned back a little. "Are you frustrated with me?"

"No, baby, I just don't want you to get hurt. What if we're misunderstanding what he was saying in his email? We don't even know he's gay."

He gave me a disbelieving look. "How many straight guys would say our picture was cute?"

"Okay, so maybe he's gay." But gay and kinky was another matter altogether.

Cooper seemed to read my mind. "I know that doesn't mean anything. A lot of people would have questions when they find out this stuff."

"We might've been just someone friendly to talk to. He made it sound like he got other emails, so maybe ours stood out."

"Because we're *cute*." Cooper's eyes sparkled. "I just had to see where it went. You're not changing your mind about wanting to find a master? You're on board with this, right?"

"Yes." I leaned in and kissed him gently. "We've talked about this for a long time and didn't rush. We know what we're looking for."

It'd taken me a lot longer than Cooper to accept what I liked and to see that having a master to interact with us as pups would be interesting. But in contrast, the idea of having a third in our relationship came pretty easily once it turned romantic. We'd both always been attracted to the same type of guy, and neither of us was that verse. We tried, but we were really both submissive bottoms even though I had a tendency to hide my preferences more.

Opening up to people was hard.

I'd played around a bit in high school, but once I picked Cooper up from his house the day he was kicked out, there hadn't been anyone else for me. And I never regretted that for a moment, but sometimes I imagined someone strong wrapping their arms around us and letting it all fade away.

It hadn't taken me long to figure out I was a bottom in bed. My earliest fantasies always leaned that way, and my first fumbling attempts with another curious guy down the street only confirmed it. Accepting the more submissive part was harder.

There was no way I could really understand what the feelings meant while I was living at home. It wasn't until we were cuddled up in the one tiny bed in the roach motel that we'd started talking and sharing about more than just who we thought was cute or what kind of guy we wanted to meet when we got out of from under our parents' noses.

Cooper, for all his sweet looks and bouncing personality, knew how to research everything dirty online. It had been a fabulous learning experience until Cooper's parents turned off his phone, and we'd lost the internet. For two teenage guys, that had been all the incentive we'd needed to get off our asses and find jobs.

God, I'd been so frightened that my planning wouldn't be enough, and that we'd starve because I wouldn't be able to support us. Cooper had taken every knock as just a bump in the road that we would get through. He'd told me repeatedly how impressed he was with my planning and how grown-up I was. As I looked around our apartment now, I could smile. Everything had turned out okay, but it had felt like we were drowning at the time.

Planning for me being on my own hadn't prepared me for what it would be like to have Cooper with me. I'd known for a long time that my dad was going to kick me out as soon as I graduated. He'd tried to do it when I turned eighteen my senior year, but once he realized the shit he could get into with the school, he backed off.

I'd mowed lawns and worked all kinds of odd jobs, saving

up every bit of money I could all through high school and had a decent amount set aside. That was the only thing that kept us safe. I had a pretty good idea of what would happen to me if I ended up on the street, and that wasn't the goal.

I was going to make something of myself just so I could shove it in my old man's face one day.

Cooper hadn't been given any warning at all. It was even crueler than knowing your family came with an expiration date. He hadn't been able to save or work on finding a job after high school. They'd kept talking to him about college and long-term career plans. It'd taken him a while to tell me what they'd found out that made them go postal.

The puppy play.

One time not clearing his internet history and everything had come crashing down around him. As scared as I'd been when I'd gotten the call, I'd also been so relieved that he'd known he could call me. I think they pictured him crawling back and promising to be the *normal* boy they really wanted, but he hadn't seen it that way. He'd said that someday they would come around and understand what a terrible decision they'd made.

He felt sorry for them.

He was a better person than I was because I'd gone back and egged their house that night while he slept in a dirty hotel room.

"Hey, you okay? You seem kind of spacey. Did you not get lunch again today?" He started to frown and gave me a stern look. "You need to—"

Laughing, I pulled him close again. "No, I was just thinking. But I did eat lunch today. *And* I started dinner. I got some chicken at the store and I even found a new recipe."

"Look at you." Cooper beamed. "Do I have enough time to get a shower before its ready?"

He didn't appreciate smelling like coffee all the time, but I loved the rich scent that followed him around. "Yes, it's baking and will be at least another half an hour."

His smile widened. "Oh, fancy, using the oven and everything."

"Only the best for you." Pulling him flush against me, I let him feel how hard my cock was. "Do you want company in the shower? I bet you could use some help making sure you're very clean."

Cooper sagged into me and started rubbing his dick against mine. "*Very* clean?"

"Very."

He gave me a little grin. "Half an hour isn't long."

"But I can wear you out in less than that, can't I? I bet you've been thinking about him all afternoon and creating the best fantasies." Cooper blushed faintly but nodded, a whimper escaping as he rubbed against me. "I bet you thought about being his pup as you served people coffee, and then imagined how he would take us both while you pretended to be the sweet, polite guy who thanked everyone for coming in. You were thinking naughty things, weren't you?"

He groaned and gave me a nod, but that wasn't enough. "Tell me what you were thinking. You want to share the fantasy with me, don't you?"

Cooper started to shake as he rutted against me. I knew it wouldn't be long until he came, so I grabbed his hips to keep him from getting there too fast. I wasn't ready for him to be done yet. As much as I wanted to be the one who was falling apart and desperate, I wanted to make it as good as I could for him. "Tell me."

"We were pups, and he was making me go through one of those obstacle courses we saw on his website. You were curled up next to him, and I was going as fast as I could. When I pleased him, he was caressing me and touching me, telling me what a good pup I was. When I was too slow, I didn't get to feel his hands on me." Cooper let out a little whimper and tried to thrust himself against me, but I held him too tightly.

"Was he petting your tail and making you feel so good?" Cooper gasped and nodded. When I was a pup, it was more about relaxing and curling into Cooper, and hopefully a master one day, but Cooper was more excitable. He loved the way the plug of the tail rubbed against his prostate, and something about the energy of chasing a toy or running around as a puppy made him horny.

But that was what was so perfect about the lifestyle. It was okay if we liked to play different ways. We needed a master who understood that. I just wasn't so sure it was safe to get our hopes up over a guy who *might* be curious but who'd never explored the fetish community before. There was a good chance he'd never even respond back, no matter how cute Cooper's email had been.

"Let's get you clean, and I'll make you feel so good. But I bet Master wouldn't be that nice. He'd make you come now then use that sexy ass in the shower too. Even though you'd already orgasmed, he'd still want to show you who you belonged to." Cooper and I weren't much for a lot of the stuff people associated with BDSM, but he loved the idea of being used and owned and made to come.

"Sawyer...you have to let me..." Cooper started pulling me close, the need to get off the only thing in his mind.

"Then shower and we'll get you...clean."

He was making needy, desperate noises, but he finally pulled away enough to start tugging me toward the bathroom. Cooper must have been fantasizing about what could happen all afternoon to be that worked up.

Some people might have felt weird knowing that their lover was thinking about someone else, but we'd gotten used to teasing each other with what our fantasy master would do. It made things easier with two subs if we could at least pretend there was a Dom there with us.

Cooper just about ran us to the small bathroom that was right beside the bedroom. Throwing open the door and turning on the shower, he started stripping off his clothes in record time. I wasn't far behind him, though I was too practical to have started imagining dirty things about someone we hadn't even met yet.

Just seeing how excited Cooper was and how much it'd turned him on got me going. Sometimes, I wished I could let go and sink into it as easily as he did. Maybe it was because he honestly saw the best in every situation, but I had a harder time picturing it working out the way we dreamed about.

As soon as I was naked, Cooper stepped into the tiny shower. It was small, but we'd had enough practice to make it work. He leaned back into the spray because he knew how much I liked watching the water drip down his body. It was the reason our shower curtain was the clear see-through kind that hid nothing. Some days, he'd get in the shower early while I was getting ready for work just to tease me before I left.

I didn't take the time to watch him like I normally would; we were both too ready. Seeing him naked, I couldn't help but remember the scrawny kid I first met. Cooper had grown taller over the years, finally getting a growth spurt after almost everyone else in our grade, but he'd never filled out. He was still on the shorter side, but it gave him a boyish, almost twinkish look I didn't think he'd ever grow out of.

His cock was long and lean, matching the rest of his body perfectly, and at that moment it was red and sticking straight out from his body, desperately begging for attention. I wrapped my hand around it as soon as I got in the shower. We took turns topping. That was the fairest way we could think of, but even though it was my turn, what I wanted more than almost anything was for his fictional master to be in there with us.

I loved Cooper desperately. He was more than a lover, more than family, but as greedy as it probably sounded, we both wanted more. As I roughly teased his cock, I imagined Master standing behind us, telling me what to do, telling me what he would touch and how he would make love to me. I pictured him taking Cooper roughly while I curled up and watched them go at it. I thought about how it would feel for us both to be able to relax and let someone else handle everything.

Until we found Master—the man that I was starting to think didn't really exist anywhere but in our heads—I was going to take care of Cooper and give him everything he needed. "Turn around so he can see that sexy ass. Master wants me to fuck you hard and make you shoot cum everywhere. Then he's going to clean his dirty boy."

He looked so innocent, but the dirty talk sent him even higher. Cooper turned himself around in the tiny space and arched out his ass while he pressed against the still-cold tiles. I couldn't resist teasing him and making him more desperate. "I don't know, Master, I'm not sure he's needy enough."

Cooper shook his head, thrusting his needy ass out even more. "Please, please, please…I'm ready…I need—*ahhh…*"

The dirty talk and his begging had given me just enough time to grab the lube off the little shelf at the back of the shower. Knowing he wanted the sting, I sank a finger deep inside him in one thrust. It wasn't much, but it was enough to make his brain shut down and his body start to shake again.

I ran my finger slowly over his prostate as I pulled it out, then pushed it back in. By the time I added a second finger, he was grasping at the smooth tiles and begging for more. From me…from our imaginary master…anyone and anything that would let him get off.

"You're showing Master what a dirty boy you are." I growled the words in his ear, doing my best to give him everything he needed.

When his head was thrown back, and his body was so ready I wasn't sure he'd be able to stand upright in the shower much longer, I moved behind him and took him in one long thrust. We hadn't used condoms in years, but the feel of his body wrapped tightly around mine still took my breath away.

"Master says you can't come until he gives you permission. He wants to use you next, and that means you have to stay hard and desperate for him." I nibbled on his ear and whispered the wicked words low.

As much as I wanted it to last, three strokes were all it took for him to explode. Cum shot over the tiles in long ropes, and he cried out as the pleasure rushed through him. His orgasm forced mine to the surface. I wanted to keep the fantasy going, but every time I watched him come, it was like my body needed to follow him.

Filling him with my cum, I couldn't help but think of all the things that could happen when we met our third. He had to be out there somewhere. Did he know what he was missing? Did he know that there were two pups out there who wanted his attention and hopefully his love?

Was I feeling a little whiny and probably tired? Yes.

Holding Cooper while we both came down, I thought about how grateful I was for the way things had turned out. Sure, there were always dreams and needs, but what we had was wonderful, and I couldn't imagine my life without him.

Would I have pushed myself the same way without having someone else to worry over? Maybe. But with him there beside me as we struggled, it had given me a reason to try harder and a desperation that wouldn't have been there on my own.

As the water started to cool, I pulled out of him and reached for the soap. "Come on. We need to get you clean before we both freeze."

"One day," he mumbled as I started scrubbing him down. "I

want us to have a big house with one of those unlimited hot water tanks."

"And a shower large enough for both of us to relax in without worrying about getting water all over the floor or someone falling." I snickered at the memories, running the washcloth over his back.

"And a bedroom that can fit a huge bed big enough for all three of us." His smile was contagious as he turned around, and I knew he could see it in his head as clearly as if it were right there in front of us.

"Yes, so big we need custom sheets like that huge one you showed me online." The average American was freakier than they were leading everyone to believe when people could come up with a thousand reasons why they needed a bed designed for a couple of football players and their lovers.

"And a living room with doggie beds and a fireplace to curl up in front of." He wrapped his arms around me as I turned us, so he would be standing directly under the water.

Cooper shivered and laughed. "It's cold."

"I told you so." Quickly washing his hair, I made sure he was rinsed as he reached to turn the water off.

"I'm starving." He leaned in and gave me a kiss before grabbing our towels off the rack. "Work was crazy busy, but I got a chance to talk with April, and she thinks that I have a good shot at the manager position when the new store opens up."

"Any hints about when that will be?" They'd been talking about the possibility of a new location for months, but the owners liked to plan things out carefully and wanted to keep the company from growing too fast.

He deflated a little. "At least another six months." Then perking up, he smiled. "But that gives me time to start working on my degree and learning more about the management side of things from April. I'll be completely ready when they start hiring for the new position."

"They'd be stupid to pick anyone else. You've been a great employee from day one, and you've made it clear you want to stay with the company and move up the ladder." Drying off, I stepped out of the tub. "Sure, they took a chance when they hired you initially, but you've more than shown them what a great job you can do."

No references, no previous employment, and living in a motel down the street, he probably hadn't come across as the most preferable candidate, but they'd hired him. I wasn't sure if they knew how grateful we'd been for him getting that job. It had been a huge weight lifted off both of us and had given Cooper a new path to focus on instead of the one that had been yanked out from under him.

He gave me a confident smile. "I'm going to show them that I'm perfect for it. And once I get it, we're going to start saving up for fun things like a vacation and a house."

"Big plans." I gave him another kiss then reached for my clothes. "What kind of vacation?" That was easier for me to picture than a house.

"The beach or one of those resorts from the commercials where everything is paid for or a cruise." He was getting excited, but all I saw were dollar signs.

"How about we think about a weekend at the beach sometime? It's not that far, and if we plan it out, we might get a good enough deal to make it work." The fears of being homeless and desperate never quite left me, so I had a tendency to be too careful with money, even after we didn't really need to worry any longer.

"That sounds perfect. The extra overtime I've been getting could go toward that. A vacation fund?" Cooper never seemed to mind my caution with our savings or my need to plan everything out. He just accepted it right away and never questioned it.

"I like that idea. Who knows? If everyone gets sick again, it might pay for a big vacation." I laughed as he threw his towel at me.

"Oh no, we're not wishing for that. I want everyone back at work." Shaking his head at me, he left the bathroom and headed for the bedroom.

"Dinner should be ready in just a minute."

His voice called out from the bedroom as I headed toward the kitchen. "I'll hurry. It smells wonderful."

I had every intention of checking on dinner because I knew the timer was going to go off any minute, but seeing my phone on the couch got me sidetracked. I told myself I'd just check one more time. Maybe he'd responded to Cooper's email.

Nothing.

Before I could set my phone down, Cooper came out of the bedroom, his tight T-shirt and loose track pants only emphasizing how lean he was. "Did he email back yet?"

"No." Not liking the way he deflated, I continued. "But it's still early. He might have evening classes or something, so he might not even be home yet."

Cooper nodded, glancing at the time on the phone. "You're right. He's probably still working. We'll check in the morning, but he it might take a few days if he's busy."

Tossing my phone back onto the couch, I nodded and reached out to pull my always-looking-on-the-bright-side lover into my arms. "You're right."

The timer went off, making him smile. "And I'm hungry too."

"Come on. Let's see if it's edible or if we need to get pizza." I wasn't as confident about my cooking skills as Cooper was.

He seemed to be offended on my behalf, because he frowned. "I'm sure it will be fabulous."

"Um, do I need to remind you about the pork chops last week? Or the roast the week before?" Cooper shook his head and refused to listen.

"Learning experiences. And we found a new website for recipes. It will be delicious." Cooper leaned in and gave me a kiss. "You need to think more positively."

He always made me smile. "That's what I have you for." Another quick kiss and I cupped his face. "I love you."

Cooper grinned. "Because I'm wonderful...of course you love me." Then he danced away out of reach. "I'm awesome. You have to love me."

"You're right. Why didn't I think of that?"

"You just needed me to remind you," he teased playfully.

"I need you for all kinds of things." The words came out slightly romantic.

"Like what?" He stopped moving away and looked at me curiously.

"Like doing the dishes since I cooked." Cooper groaned and reached down to throw one of the couch cushions at me.

"That's terrible."

"But you love me anyway." I grinned. "Food. And no throwing things in the house. Master will think we've got terrible manners."

He laughed. "But then he might punish us."

There was that. Spankings were only so much fun when you'd rather be the one getting them. "Maybe he'll punish us both."

Cooper nodded. "Because you started it, you'd have to be punished too. It's only fair."

It would be perfect.

Now all we had to do was find Master Right.

6

COOPER

The alarm would go off in just a few minutes, but I was still trying to sneak out from under Sawyer's arm and escape the bed. I had to be in earlier than usual, but that wasn't the reason I was inching along, trying not to wake him.

Showers and coffee would be coming shortly, but what I wanted more than anything was to check my email. And I knew from prior experience that playing with my phone in bed would wake him up. Something about the light, however low, got Sawyer's brain going.

I didn't want his brain going. I wanted his too-realistic outlook still asleep while I daydreamed about emails and what might be coming. I wasn't really expecting an email to be waiting for us. When it wasn't there after dinner, I realized that it might take Jackson a few days to figure out what he wanted, or at the very least, what he wanted to say.

Figuring out that they were interested in something kinky could throw anyone for a loop.

And he was clearly interested.

Just the fact that he'd written back said it loud and clear. And then there was the whole "cute" thing. Our first email made sure that he knew exactly what we were looking for. The only reason he'd continue to contact us was if it interested him on some level.

I hoped it was enough to keep him communicating.

I was almost free of the bed and just trying to carefully pull the covers off when Sawyer's arms wrapped around me. "The alarm hasn't even gone off, Coop."

His exasperated voice was still filled with exhaustion, and I was mentally throwing around curse words. "Shhh, go back to sleep. I just have to use the bathroom."

"Bullshit." His arms tightened even more. "You want to check your email."

Damn it.

"Maybe? It's something I normally do over coffee, so that would make sense." I was a terrible liar. "Get a little more rest. I'll have the coffee ready when you get up."

Twenty minutes wasn't much time for him to get real sleep in, but it would give me time to check both email accounts and start the coffee. That had been one of the first things we'd bought for ourselves when we'd finally moved out of the motel.

Sawyer had been incredibly excited to have something better than the crappy stuff that was always available in the lobby, and I'd been grateful for stronger caffeine because he was not a morning person.

"You owe me big time." He grumbled and rolled onto me, pinning me to the bed. "I want the good coffee you make with the stuff in it."

He was lucky I was a morning person because that sentence wasn't terribly descriptive. Thankfully, I knew what "the stuff" was. "Deal."

"Okay." He groaned and rolled off, giving me a kiss on the forehead. "I'll be out in just a minute. And no checking emails until I get there."

Someone was grumpy this morning. Sleep was only part of

it, though. I knew he worried about me being disappointed, but I understood that Jackson was going to need time. He'd let us know when he was ready. I could feel it.

"Don't be disappointed if he doesn't email yet." I leaned in and gave him a kiss as I climbed out. "It's okay if it takes him a while."

Sawyer coughed and shook his head, peeking one eye open in the early morning light. "Okay, I'll try."

No matter how tough and cool he tried to play, he felt things as strongly as I did. He'd just pushed the emotions away and had been disappointed over so many things for so long, he'd gotten used to hiding it. But he had me to watch over him. I gave him one last kiss on the cheek. "We're not in a rush. We can give him some time."

One side of his mouth turned up in a lopsided grin. "You're right."

"And Mr. Smart and Sexy is going to make coffee." I smiled when he barked out a laugh.

"Sexy, huh?"

"That's what you were saying last night." By the time we'd crawled into bed the previous evening, I'd recovered from our shower fun and had done my best to make Sawyer feel as good as I had.

I wasn't the world's best top, but he'd been crying out in pleasure by the end and had gone off like a rocket, so I thought I'd done a pretty good job. Laughing, I scrambled away as he tried to grab me. With his dark hair going everywhere and the sleepy, needy look starting to fill his eyes, I knew we'd get distracted if I let him catch me.

And as incredible as that sounded, I wasn't sure he could manage morning sex in only a few minutes. Quickies were great, but in the morning, Sawyer liked to take his time. That would have to wait until we didn't have work.

As I just about bounced out of the room excitedly, he was

still grumbling and had a death grip on the covers. It was going to take him a few minutes to make his way out of bed, but I didn't dawdle in the bathroom. No, I was in and out as fast as I could and then hurried to start the coffee.

History had taught me that the smell would get him out of bed faster than almost anything else. He was like a character from one of those old cartoons where the smell of food carried them down the hall. Coffee or bacon would both work perfectly for it.

Unfortunately, there was no bacon, and no time to make it anyway, so coffee all done up with "the stuff," as he'd put it, would have to do. By the time he came stumbling into the kitchen, still not much more awake than he had been when I'd left him in bed, I had his coffee waiting and my email app ready to open.

I hadn't even peeked.

The temptation was getting stronger though, so it was a good thing he'd walked in when he did. Sawyer flopped down in his seat and sighed as he inhaled the aroma before taking his first sip of the coffee and chocolate concoction that he loved.

"Can I open it now?" It was like a present sitting there in front of me, and I couldn't wait to look at it. Never mind the fact that it might be empty—that didn't matter.

Sawyer shook his head, clearly not understanding my excitement, and nodded. I didn't take his silence personally. I'd seen him when we had absolutely no coffee in the house, so this was nothing. I was already halfway through my cup, so I pushed it aside and grabbed my phone.

I finally got another laugh out of him when it almost went flying, and I'd barely caught it in time. Swiping my finger across the screen, I tapped on the email app and quickly shifted over to the secondary email account.

"Yes!" Jackpot.

Sawyer stared at me in shock before he finally spoke. "He actually emailed back?"

"Yes." I couldn't help grinning.

No matter what it said, he'd answered back.

I couldn't tell from the preview section if it was what I was hoping to see or not. From the look of it, at least he'd read my email because I could see him talking about being a pet owner. Had he taken it *too* literally? Trying to subtly take a deep breath and calm down, I clicked on the message.

"Oh!" I'd been afraid he would respond so businesslike that I wouldn't be able to tell if he was interested or not, but his curiosity was clear. Sawyer watched me, sipping his coffee, refusing to get his hopes up. "Listen to this part. 'You might find that they are more curious than they would expect when they start getting more information.' He's actually curious about the lifestyle!"

"And this part! '...but just from what I've seen online, it's a little confusing.' He's looking up puppy play online!" I couldn't believe it. "And he asks a question. That means he wants a reply, right?"

Sawyer seemed to finally get frustrated with my random bits of email thrown at him. He started grumbling and grabbed my phone out of my hand. "Hey! I'm not done."

"Then you should have read the whole thing out loud to begin with." As he started reading, still curled around his coffee, Sawyer's body relaxed, and I could see his mind racing as he read the email. It took so long he had to have read it twice before he gave me the phone back.

"What do you think?" My mind was dancing around in circles, and I couldn't help but smile. Jackson was curious and still wanted to talk to us. He was even making sure he understood what we were looking for, and that had to be significant.

"I don't know." He was looking at the phone like it was a Transformer and would start moving on its own any minute.

"Come on…" I moved my chair around, so he could see the screen again too. "He's interested in learning more about the lifestyle, and he wanted to clarify how we saw the master in our relationship. I don't think it's just a casual question for him. He's never said anything rude or sexual. He's curious."

"But what happens if he doesn't like what he finds as he starts looking into the lifestyle more?" Sawyer tried to sound calm, but I could hear the undercurrent of emotion.

"I don't think he would've emailed back if what he was seeing scared him off." I leaned my head against Sawyer's shoulder. "He seems like he's thinking this through."

Sawyer gave a hesitant nod. "And he admits that someone new would have a lot of questions."

"See, that's a good thing. I'd be worried if he didn't understand that part." Just the fact that he realized there was a lot to learn made me feel better. I didn't want some cocky master who was just starting to figure out the scene and thought he knew everything. I liked that Sawyer and I had worked our way through it together.

I wanted a master who would love us and take care of us, but I wasn't expecting perfection. There would be a learning curve, and being with our master while he started discovering it would make it even more special.

I liked the idea of us being the first pups he'd play with.

I'd been the first person Sawyer ever loved and the first person he'd let see him vulnerable. Trying the puppy play and opening up to it hadn't been easy for him. And he'd been my first everything really, so the idea of being our master's first pups made it seem even more wonderful. Being the first guys he slid tails into. Being the first men he petted and threw the ball for. There were so many firsts I pictured having with our master.

Sawyer looked from me to the phone again. "Do you want to email him back, or should I?"

I couldn't tell if he was hinting or not, so I started poking at the question. "Would it make you uncomfortable to do it?"

"I don't think so." He picked up his mug and took another drink. "But your emails sound more friendly." He set the cup down and chuckled. "Mine sound like I'm planning out business meetings."

"I don't mind emailing him back." I loved the idea of getting to know him more, and I had a thousand questions running through my head. "How about in the next email, I see if he wants to talk on the phone?"

"In person?" He must have realized how odd that question sounded because he shook his head like he was clearing it and tried again. "I mean...well, I don't know exactly what I mean, but that just seems like a big jump."

Did it?

"Eventually, we're going to have dinner with him or something to move things along. Once we talk to him and figure out if he's really interested and if there's any chemistry there. But yeah, in person." We'd talked about what we wanted to happen when we finally found someone that felt right. Was he not remembering the same conversations I did?

"What if he meets us and changes his mind? Like, it's all just too much for him." Sawyer tried to look relaxed as he picked up his coffee, but I knew what was running through his mind. Getting rejected again wasn't something he was willing to deal with.

"Then I'll make sure he's okay with things before we meet. And I really think that we'll be able to tell the chemistry part when we talk on the phone. I think once he's more comfortable with what we're throwing at him, then he'll be a little more take-charge. This is new to him, so he probably doesn't want to come across as weird or something." I wasn't really sure what he was thinking, but it made sense to me. I wouldn't want to come across creepy or stalkery when I was trying to get to know a couple of kinky guys.

Ménage...kink...new people in general...yeah, I could see how that would make him cautious.

Sawyer's concern seemed to only get worse when I said I would figure things out. "But I don't want you to get hurt."

"I realize this might not work. But I feel okay about it all because if we find one guy who's interested and is even considering what we're looking for, then there will be other ones out there. Where there is one potentially kinky dog trainer who likes the idea of dating two sexy guys, then there will be others."

"There will, huh?" Sawyer laughed.

"Of course." It would just take time to find him. "We just have to look longer for him."

Sawyer nodded, but the way his lips quirked up on one side let me know he thought I was crazy. "We're young and not in a rush."

I shrugged. "Maybe a little bit of a rush. That big bed I showed you online was awesome." Then I grinned. "You hog the covers."

"Hey!" He pulled back enough that I had to sit up. "If anyone steals the covers, it's you. I'm just defending myself."

Bullshit. "Very preemptively then."

"Such snark." Sawyer wagged a finger at me. "Master wouldn't like that tone."

I grinned. "Then he can spank me to make me behave."

Sawyer did a good job when he played the Dom and put me over his lap, but it wasn't the same as knowing a real master was thoroughly enjoying making my ass hot and needy. We both knew Sawyer would rather be on the other end too.

It was another way I knew how much he loved me.

"And you for starting it. You teased me first."

His shocked expression was purely for fun. "You'd tattle on me?"

I nodded enthusiastically. "Of course, because you'd love it."

Okay, so maybe we'd be a little bit of a handful for Master. I knew we'd be worth it, though. We just had to find him, so we could show him. "Now hurry up and caffeinate. You have to go to work first and I have an email to put together."

He grinned. "Not going to wait until after work to email him back?"

"Hell, no. I don't have that kind of willpower. I'd die." And I'd be so excited and distracted that I'd mix up orders all day long. Nope, I wasn't going to set myself up for failure.

Sawyer was laughing so hard he gave up trying to drink his coffee. Pushing back from the table, he stood up and bent over to give me a kiss. "I'm going to finish getting ready then find breakfast. Have fun emailing Jackson."

"I will." My smile was so big it hurt my cheeks. He'd emailed us back. I was going to hold on to that thought all day long. No matter what happened, he was interested enough and curious enough to put himself out there.

My coffee looked too cold to drink, so I stood up and followed him out of the kitchen. "Did we leave the computer on the couch?"

My parents hadn't let me take my computer, but I had my phone, so we hadn't been completely cut off. But when they'd turned that off, it'd certainly felt like we were isolated from everything. Now we had unlimited internet and smartphones and I was going to college soon. Some people took those things for granted, but I was always going to see them as proof of our hard work.

We could do *anything* we set our minds to.

"I think so." He turned and glanced down at the phone in my hand. "You know you can email him back on that."

"Smartass." The keyboard was too small to type out a long

letter, and I wasn't planning on cutting it short. I had questions, and I wanted to tell him more about us because he had to be curious.

Sawyer wiggled his ass and dropped his pants to moon me as he went into the bathroom. I was still laughing when he shut the door to keep the heat in and started the water. Booting up the computer, I couldn't help but wonder what Jackson would think of us. Would we end up being too silly for him?

"No, we'd keep him young. Masters need someone to make them laugh." As I finally signed in to our email account, I glanced over at the clock. I had a few minutes, but not long enough to dawdle, so as soon as I hit the reply button, I started to type. He wouldn't want planned out and perfect; he'd want to see the real me, anyway.

HI, JACKSON!

I have to confess I was glad you emailed us back. I know it's something different than what you're used to, and I was excited to see that you've been looking puppy play up online. What do you think of it so far? Sawyer was a little hesitant and confused when I first showed it to him, so I get that it's hard to understand.

Yes, Sawyer and I are looking for a master to be a third in our relationship. I don't think it's oversharing to tell you that we're both bottoms and looking for a top as well as a master (Sawyer's going to complain and tell me that's oversharing lol but he won't see this until later, so that's okay). I have to confess that we looked up your business online. Was that you on the site? It made it look like it was you, so I hope I'm not telling one of your employees that he's cute but well, you're cute. Sawyer thinks so too.

I was curious about the types of guys you usually date (Sawyer probably is too, but he didn't say anything specifically). Have you ever dated two guys at the same time? Are you a take things slow kind of guy or do you like to move faster? Would dating two guys bother you? If you haven't guessed, I have lots of questions. Would you like to chat on the phone sometime (I'm hinting that sometime means soon lol just in case you couldn't tell)?

I haven't dated much. Sawyer and I got together just after high school, and we've been a family ever since. Does it bother you that we're younger? Not jailbait, though. Sawyer says I look young and made us take the picture a dozen times until I looked old enough that it wouldn't freak someone out. Got to head to work, but hopefully we'll talk soon.

Bye!

Cooper

HITTING THE SEND BUTTON, I DIDN'T EVEN READ IT THROUGH or second-guess how I came across. I didn't hide things from Sawyer or censor myself, and I wasn't going to pretend to be anything I wasn't for someone we were getting to know.

Shutting the computer, I took a deep breath and looked at the clock. Time to grab food and start to get ready for the day. The water had just turned off. I knew if I hurried, I'd have enough time to make eggs for Sawyer. So I climbed off the couch, trying not to think about Jackson.

Keeping him out of my mind all day was going to be hard, though. Waiting to see what he said in his reply would make me crazy. But I couldn't spend all day worrying.

He was either going to love us for who we were, or it wasn't meant to be. I just had to keep reminding myself of that.

7

JACKSON

He'd emailed back.

I probably shouldn't have been surprised. I'd grabbed my phone to check my email before I'd even gotten out of bed, so I wasn't sure why I expected him to be any different. It wasn't like he was trying to play games and keep me guessing.

As I lay there reading, the mental image that came up had me picturing a bouncy little thing that *might* have been slightly over-caffeinated. Either that, or he really was as excitable as Sawyer had hinted in his first letter.

Reading his list of questions, I had to smile. He'd gotten right to the point. No small talk or useless questions just to ease into things. I liked it. The straightforward nature of the words made me think that he was taking it as seriously as I was.

Maybe that wasn't the right way to phrase it, but when I'd stayed up half the night researching different aspects of a potential relationship, there didn't seem to be another word for it. Sure, I wanted passion and for there to be a connection, but I wasn't going to jump into something serious without knowing what they were looking for and how I felt about their needs. Just the fact that I'd been reading online long enough to get sober said something about how drawn I was to them.

Reading through the letter again, I couldn't decide my opinion on the phone conversation idea. With any other potential date, I would have already mentioned talking on the phone. But it seemed like a huge step.

Which was ridiculous.

A phone call or, hell, going totally crazy and asking them out to dinner would be simple and easy. But would that really let me know if I could handle everything? Would talking at dinner show me what it would be like to get serious with two men? Would talking on the phone help me to understand how the puppy play would really feel?

No matter what I decided, anything would be more helpful than emails back and forth.

Shoving back the covers, I set my phone down and told myself it was time to start getting ready for the day. Even though I'd slept in, completely blowing off the mental note I'd made to work on the books before classes started, I still had plenty of time to get ready.

I had a handful of early classes during the week, but most of my work was in the evenings and on the weekends. I'd dated a few guys who hadn't liked working around my schedule, but I loved what I was doing and wouldn't have it any other way.

Grabbing some clothes as I headed into the bathroom, I tried to remind myself why I liked having my work and home so close together. It was nice in the evenings when all I had to do was lock up the warehouse-style building on the edge of the property where I held classes and walk across the lawn to the house, but it sucked when it meant putting clothes on first thing.

Little old ladies who came at ungodly hours to pay their bills did not need to know that I slept naked. So clothes first thing was important. I'd only had one surprise where I'd needed to scramble for something to wear before I'd learned that lesson.

Dressed and ready for the day in about fifteen minutes, I headed through the house and into the kitchen. When I'd first had the house built a few years ago, everyone had said that I'd never use all the square footage, but as I looked at the guest rooms and large living room, I couldn't help but think that the house would be great for three people.

The practical side of me said everyone would have enough space for their own office or just a bedroom they could use to escape and make it their own. I'd read an article during my marathon research session that talked about how important it was for the different couples to have private time together and for the individuals to have places they could retreat to.

Well, the house had that in spades. I just wasn't sure how I felt about everything else I'd read in that piece. Different people needed different amounts of personal space; I got that. But when the couple…threesome…group that was living together talked about pairing off and doing things as a couple, that had seemed harder to follow.

How would I feel if Cooper and Sawyer went to the movies without me, or how would Sawyer feel if Cooper and I went out to dinner? There were so many parts that I just couldn't see, and figuring out how I felt about them was almost impossible.

I had a feeling it was something that I wouldn't understand until I was in the situation, but was that fair to them? Could I get to know them and possibly enter into a relationship when I didn't even know how I would feel about the practical side of things? We'd know pretty quickly if we clicked or not, so the chemistry part didn't worry me…it was everything else that did.

The kitchen was another room that was too big for just me, but when I pictured three people getting breakfast in the morning or helping to make dinner, the space was perfect. It had an old-fashioned feel, but with nice appliances and tons of countertop. I had to admit that I thought I'd done a great job on it.

The house had a lot of woodwork that gave it an older feel —but with newer furniture and things that balanced it out and kept it from looking like old people lived there. As I made the coffee, looking out at the backyard, trying to imagine what Sawyer and Cooper would think of everything, I heard a car door slam.

A quick look at the calendar on the wall said I didn't have any lessons that I'd forgotten. I wasn't sure who it could be. Most of my friends worked more traditional jobs, so they'd been at work for a couple of hours at least.

That left family.

If I was lucky, it might be a door-to-door salesman who was very lost.

Nope, no such luck. The back door opened, and Melissa's face popped around the opening. "Good morning. I'd say afternoon since it's getting close, but you don't look like you've been up that long." She looked around curiously before shutting the door. "Should I have knocked?"

"Yes, but because it's basic manners. No one else is here."

"You know, if you start dating your kinky cuties then I'm going to have to knock and give everyone time to get clothes on." Melissa grinned and started heading over to the coffeepot.

If my imagination was anywhere close to correct, she was right.

Melissa glanced over as she doctored her coffee. "Still emailing your new friends?"

"Yes, but Cooper emailed first thing this morning that he wants to talk on the phone. But I'm thinking that dinner might be an easier way to talk to both of them at the same time."

She shook her head. "You're like an old man when it comes to technology. There are all kinds of ways you could talk without going on a date."

I shrugged and took a sip of my coffee. "Maybe, but I want to be able to see them as we talk and get a feel for how we interact. I don't think the phone is the best way to handle it."

"So you're serious about the whole idea?" She took a sip and leaned against the counter.

"Why? Should I not be?" They were sweet and cute, and even the few emails we'd exchanged felt more personal than my last couple of dates.

"I'm not saying don't consider it." She started wandering around the kitchen before settling down at the table. "I just think that puppy play is a very different lifestyle than you've been exposed to."

That didn't mean it was scary.

"I was basically unfamiliar with the lifestyle, yes." Aside from a few odd TV shows and maybe some online videos that I wouldn't have originally thought were real, I hadn't given it much thought.

She studied me and took another drink of her coffee. "Are you becoming more familiar with it?"

"Yes."

"What are you thinking?" The way she asked the question felt like I should have been laid out on a couch in a therapist's office.

"Are we really going to have this discussion?" Rolling my eyes, I didn't try to hide that I was starting to get frustrated with the interrogation.

She cocked one eyebrow. "Do you have anyone else to talk to about this shit?"

Good point.

"I think I have enough of the caretaker qualities that the lifestyle would not be a bad fit. I also like the playful energy that comes from dogs, and the actual act of playing is familiar. I would have to think that the same things would carry over when the puppy isn't actually a dog." I thought it might. Maybe.

She gave me a skeptical look. "I think the basic question is simple. Did the videos and stuff you watched—not porn, real people—give you those warm fuzzy feelings that made it seem like a good idea? Turned-on doesn't really matter because not all puppy play is sexual. In fact, a lot isn't, but can you see curling up with a pup and petting them? Those are basic things your pup will need from a master."

That was a very good question.

I had time to think since I'd first gotten their email, and nothing I'd seen or read scared me off. I was starting to find that I wasn't as vanilla as I'd originally assumed. It seemed like I'd already been moving in a less traditional direction and this was just taking it further.

I liked taking control in bed, light restraints, and even spankings weren't out of the ordinary. I'd just never really thought of them as BDSM. I liked being able to cuddle my partner and relax with them, and I wasn't sure if what they were wearing would matter.

So what if they had a tail and collar while we watched TV on the couch?

"Nothing that I've seen was overwhelming or put me off, but it's hard to imagine how it will feel since we haven't met yet. If I'm playing what-if, and I try to picture someone from a previous relationship, then I'd have to say a solid maybe. There were a few guys who were leaning more toward the submissive end of the spectrum, but I never really considered that when I was dating someone." I probably should have.

In my defense, when I first started dating, there were more guys in the closet than out, and BDSM was nowhere near as mainstream as it was turning out to be. I grew up in the south. Not the small-town stereotype people thought of, but still Southern enough that aside from a little bit of curious stuff going on behind closed doors, most people gay, straight, or anything else were kind of boring.

She gave me another long look. "You need to be honest with them about your experience and what you're thinking. Don't let them walk into even a date without you explaining that it doesn't freak you out, but you can't visualize it and have no idea how it will feel. Give them a chance to back out if they're looking for someone with experience."

"I've been very honest with my lack of experience in this area. I've also let them know that I have questions, and I'm not ready to jump into those types of things right away." I wasn't stupid.

"Did you hint or did you actually spell it out?"

"I was polite and careful but not making it difficult to understand." There was no way they could have missed reading between the lines. And I'd been very clear that I didn't have any experience with that type of kink.

"They're submissives, Jackie. They're not looking for you to dance around a topic because you're trying not to upset the current drama queen. They're looking for someone to take charge and let them turn over the decisions to someone else." Now it was her turn to roll her eyes.

Guys always said they liked someone who took charge, but I'd yet to meet one who really did. "I don't date drama queens."

She laughed so hard coffee sprayed all over the table. When she finally caught her breath, she shook her head. "That's all you date. Crazy guys who want attention but not *too* much because then you're hovering. It's like you were trying to find someone that wasn't just like you, but you went looking in the wrong direction."

I liked taking charge when given the option, but most people, especially guys I'd dated made it seem like a minefield. "Bullshit. A guy says he's looking for someone who knows what they want or who's more alpha, but the first time you do something as simple as pick a damn restaurant instead of playing the 'What do you want?' game then they go postal."

69

She laughed. "Not if the guy is a real submissive and not just trying to play one because it's popular, or they think it sounds cool. A true submissive would be relieved to know what would make you happy. Yes, they're going to have opinions and things that they'd want too, but just knowing what would please you feels wonderful to them."

Melissa took a sip of her coffee and leaned back in the chair. "I interviewed this guy one time, so I could understand more about what my character might be thinking. He came across feisty and interesting and had lots of opinions, but when we were talking, he said he loved it when he knew exactly what his master liked or wanted. His master might not always get it, no matter what it was, but it was a weight off his shoulders not to have to guess."

"I think I'm just going to have to sit down with them and really get to know what they're looking for. What kind of master they're picturing and what kind of third they're imagining aren't things I'm going to be able to understand until we're talking about them."

She nodded. "Emails and written communication are good for spelling things out. However, these aren't questions you can answer in yes or no format like you were filling in the blanks on a school test."

"No, these are definitely essays."

She chuckled. "Agreed. And you're more of a physical person, so just imagining it probably isn't helpful for you, anyway."

Melissa was right; to really understand something, I needed to be able to touch it and experience it. Learning in school was harder because of it—my job now was perfect for it. "But if I tell them that I won't really understand how it feels until I'm actually doing it, they're going to think I'm some kind of a perv or just leading them on."

"It's going to depend on how you tell them. I'd talk about

the research and the questions you have and then get to know them for a while. By the time you actually know if there could be something between the three of you, I think you'll be able to go into the puppy play with a different mindset." Melissa was watching me, a serious expression on her face.

"What do you mean?"

She took a moment, and I could see her mind working. "Any kind of healthy BDSM or lifestyle relationship generally gets serious faster than more traditional ones. You have to be a lot more open and honest with your partner or, in this case, partners. That honesty and sharing pulls people together. By the time you're ready to delve into the puppy play, you're either going to be half in love with them and really open to making it work, or you're going to know they're not the right people for you, so it won't matter."

She touched on pieces that I'd read, but somehow, I hadn't looked at it that way. If it were someone I was already falling in love with that wanted me to try, I would. If I was honest, I had to say that of the guys I'd dated and the relationships I'd tried to make work, I hadn't been in love with that many. Looking back to those first relationships that I'd fallen so hard in, I think I would have done almost anything for them.

That was such a long time ago, though, and I was a different person now.

"Thank you, Mellie." I wasn't ready to answer her unasked question, but I wanted her to know I appreciated her insight. "Now, besides coming over for free coffee, why are you here?"

"I took the morning off because I had some stuff to get done. And I was curious to know how things were going with your cuties." She shrugged. "This is going to make a great book if you guys work it all out."

"Gross." I shuddered. "I don't want to picture you writing about my love life."

She laughed. "How do you know I haven't already used you

as inspiration? You could already be a clueless Dom or a sub who's not how everyone thinks they should look."

"That's just cruel. I show up in one of your books, and I'll definitely tell. Mom doesn't even like us posting pictures or anything remotely personal on social media. What's she going to do if you end up putting me in a book?" I gave her a wicked grin.

Melissa groaned. "She'll kill me."

"Yup." I smirked, and she balled up a napkin and threw it at me.

"You're a terrible brother."

"I know." I didn't fight my grin. I was going to milk it for all it was worth when it finally came out. If she was making as much as she'd hinted, I couldn't see her working a traditional nine-to-five much longer. She was pretty vocal about being bored stiff at her job, so if she was that close to an out, she'd take it sooner or later.

"All right, I have to go."

"Gossip and coffee then you leave."

"Yup." Now it was her turn to smirk. "And I was helpful. Don't forget that point, because if you out me, then I'm going to brag to her about how much I helped you find the men of your dreams."

"I'd still be in love and you'd be the liar. I'm going to come out on top no matter how you explain it." I wasn't going to let her forget it.

"Ass." She grinned as she started to rise.

"Aww, I love you too." Grabbing our mugs, I started taking hers over to the sink and mine to get a refill. I had work to do and an email to write. Caffeine was a must. "Now shoo. My to-do list is insane, and unless you want to be volunteered for paying bills and going over the business finances, you should escape while you can."

"Have fun emailing back your cuties." She gave a teasing

wave as she started heading out the back door.

"Go." I was picturing writing the actual email as more stressful than fun, but the idea of getting to know them better was appealing. "And knock next time!"

Laughing, she shut the door as she walked out, not making any promises. I was going to have to start remembering to lock the doors. Especially if they came over. The thought of her walking in while we were doing *anything* was horrifying.

I'd definitely end up in a book just so she could tease me about it forever.

Heading out into the living room, I grabbed my laptop and plopped down on the couch. Email first, or I wouldn't be able to focus on anything else. The beginning of the email was going to come easily. All I had to do was answer Cooper's questions, but I still wasn't sure what I was going to do about taking things to the next step.

Should I just agree to a phone call, or did I want to push for something more?

There was a part of me that wanted to agree with what he'd suggested and let them set the pace. But with what Melissa had said, I thought I would do better by listening to the bossy piece of me that I'd gotten used to ignoring. He was very insistent.

COOPER,

YES, THAT'S ME ON THE WEBSITE. THANK YOU FOR THE compliment. I'll admit that I was a little bit hesitant about how you would see me because I'm not anywhere near your age. I've dated people that were younger and some that were older, so I don't think that matters to me. I've never dated two guys at the same time, though.

I DON'T THINK I HAVE A PROBLEM WITH THE TYPE OF relationship you're looking for, because I've done some research about polyamorous relationships, and I think I'm getting a better hold on how they work. It's probably like the puppy play and not something I'm going to understand until I get to know you both more. I've also been looking that up online too. I was aware of the lifestyle before, but I guess I never stopped to consider it because I'm learning a lot.

GETTING TO KNOW YOU GUYS AND TO UNDERSTAND HOW YOU see a future relationship with someone is what I'm focusing on right now. I've never worried about going too slow or too fast before. Every relationship has been different, but since you guys have been honest that you're looking for something serious, I think I'll keep an open mind and see what feels right. Who knows? We could go out to dinner, and you guys might decide that I'm too boring to want to hang out with anymore.

TALKING ON THE PHONE SOUNDS LIKE A GOOD IDEA. I'M going to put my cell number at the bottom of the letter. If you want to give me a call later tonight, that would be great. I have classes until seven though, so calling around eight is probably a better idea. As long as the phone call goes well, I'd like to invite you guys out to dinner on Saturday. My treat so we can get to know each other better. Talk it over with Sawyer, and see what he thinks. Work's calling so I have to go, but I'm looking forward to the call.

JACKSON

Deciding not to overthink it, I quickly typed my phone number and hit the send button before closing the laptop. They were both probably busy anyway, so obsessing over the email and how they would reply would only make me crazy. If everything worked out, they might not even email back, anyway. The more I started thinking about the possibility of a phone call later, the better it sounded.

Forcing myself off the couch, I started mentally shifting gears to focus on my list for the day. The computer was calling, and what I really wanted to do was focus on the research and trying to understand what they might need from a master — from *me* one day.

At least, that was how it was starting to feel.

8

SAWYER

After seeing that Jackson had responded to our email, everything else about my day was shot. Not that I'd opened it. Cooper had made me promise that neither of us would read the email until we both got home. Well, that promise had been made hours ago, and I was starting to lose my patience.

I tried to make dinner when I got home, but my brain wasn't functioning enough to figure out what I could cook from the list of things we had in the house. So I'd gone out and grabbed a pizza. Driving there instead of getting delivery killed some of the remaining time until Cooper got off work, so it was the only thing that saved my sanity.

"Cooper."

"Sawyer!"

The minute the door opened our voices called out at the same time. Cooper bounced into the kitchen, a huge grin on his face. "He emailed back!"

"I know. I've been waiting hours to read it." Not wanting to appear too eager, I pointed to the table. "Do you want to eat first or check his message?"

He looked at me like I wasn't fooling anyone. "Come on." Taking my hand, he marched us out to the living room and grabbed the laptop before going to the couch.

Smiling, I sat down while he curled into me, balancing the computer on our laps. "This will work better. You'll want to see too."

"I will?"

Cooper snorted and started logging into the website. It only took seconds to pull the email up, but by the time he was clicking on the links, we were both holding our breaths. I'd read Cooper's email at lunch and he'd made me laugh, but I wasn't sure that Jackson would actually answer his questions.

I also wasn't sure I wanted to know the answers. But they weren't as bad as I feared they would be. "He's not scared off by the idea of two guys or two pups."

"And he wants to go out to dinner this weekend!" Cooper's eyes were wide, and he had an ear-to-ear grin. Most of the time I forgot he hadn't really dated in high school, but then he'd do something so cute or get excited, and it would remind me how different things had been for him.

Not that he'd been the type in high school to randomly hook up with some curious football player or to play doctor with a kid down the street. No, Cooper might be kinky, but he'd always had this innocence about him that made people shy away from shit like that.

"You want to go on a date with Jackson?" I laughed when Cooper did a fabulous impression of a bobblehead doll and nearly sprang up off the couch.

Remembering the computer on his lap at the last second was the only thing that kept him in place. "Yes! Do you?"

There was no way I'd say no to all that enthusiasm, even if I had reservations. But there weren't as many fears in the back of my head as I expected. Maybe if he'd been more flippant or had treated Cooper's questions more casually, it would have been different, but he seemed to be very conscious of the fact that it was serious for us, and that it wasn't a game he was playing.

Some people might think it was a little transactional or not as romantic to talk everything out by email, but I liked the distance it gave us. Jackson was right that the next step needed to be dinner. The phone call would let us know if there was some basic compatibility, but it was too easy to read into things on the phone. In person was really the only way to see how we related to each other.

Maybe I was too cautious, but I didn't want Cooper hurt. Dragging things out by email only to find out that he'd lied about something, or that we didn't have that passion for each other in person would only be harder for him. No, dinner would be better.

"What if he likes you better? What if he thinks I'm too young-looking or excitable?" Cooper's brows pulled together and he frowned, glancing down at the email.

We'd run into a few guys who'd liked one of us better than the other, and one asshole who'd said that Cooper was too bouncy. He wanted a more mature pup and hadn't tried to hide that from Cooper.

"He's already seen you're excitable. I read that last email, Mr. I'm Going To Overshare." Leaning into him, I gave him a kiss. "And he's seen a picture of both of us, so I don't see how either of those things could happen."

It had been one of the reasons I'd wanted to send a picture in the original email. Yeah, we seemed less like a scam when you could see what we looked like, but he'd also know if we weren't his type right away.

Sometimes things changed over time and people grew to love or even desire each other, but that wasn't what we were looking for. I didn't want something forced or that we'd grow into. I wanted someone to hold us, and for the passion to be there from the get-go.

Cooper started to relax, nodding to himself. "Yes, you're right."

"Of course I am." I grinned as Cooper cuddled into me, and some of my stress faded away. Jackson knew I was more reserved—that had to be obvious from the emails—and as long as you could ignore the fact that sometimes Cooper seemed young, we both looked like our pictures.

Everything was going to be fine.

"Pizza now, so we're not eating when we call?" Cooper glanced over at the pizza and back to me.

"Sure. I just got back with it, so it shouldn't be cold."

"Great, I'm starving. I think I ran a thousand miles behind the counter this afternoon." Setting the computer on the coffee table, Cooper stood up. "I'm so glad he didn't want to wait a few more days before we talked."

"I don't think you could've waited a few more *hours*." My laughter turned into a grunt when he landed on my lap.

Straddling my legs, Cooper ground his cock onto mine. It was impossible to miss that we were both already half-hard. He started kissing down my neck, and I could hear the change in his breathing as he got even more worked up. "You're not fooling me. I know that you were thinking about what he would say all afternoon, and I bet you've been going crazy waiting."

Hiding my need wasn't an option. "I looked at the preview a thousand times this afternoon."

"He's going to think we're both sexy and fabulous, and he's going to end up being perfect for us." Cooper's tongue flicked out and started teasing my ear, making me gasp. "He's going to flirt with us at dinner and get to know us, and then at the end of the night we're going to get a sexy goodnight kiss."

Cooper's teeth nibbled at the sensitive shell of my ear and his hot breath made me shiver. "You want a goodnight kiss from Master, don't you? I bet you want to see me get a kiss too. Do you think he'll be a gentleman and keep it nice and sweet, or do you think he'll take control and make it deep and dirty?"

Either. Both. The images Cooper was putting in my head were making me crazy. "I don't—Cooper—harder."

He giggled and moved his body back just enough to stop the delicious pressure on my dick. "But we need to get dinner first. Master's going to be ready in just a few minutes. He's finishing up his stuff right now, and I bet he's counting the minutes until we call."

"Master's going to punish you if you tease him like that."

"You think so?" Cooper seemed to love the idea. "What kind of punishment?"

Laughing, I refused to reward the little flirt. "Pizza."

I got a pout, but he climbed off my lap, so he really must have been hungry. Cooper started walking over to the table and glanced back at me. "You really think he's going to like us?"

"Yes. He wouldn't have taken the time to respond back if he didn't see possibilities with us." I wasn't going to magically turn into Cooper, but I was going to do my best not to imagine the worst. Jackson had been spending a lot of time researching things, if his emails were honest, and nothing he'd seen seemed to scare him off, so I had to think that was a good sign.

Cooper gave me a teasing grin. "Because we're wonderful." He amped up the smile and batted his eyelashes at me. "And we're sexy pups, so he won't be able to think of anything else but us."

"All right, wonder pup, I like the way you think, but I'm starving—so you need to feed me before your perfect master starts getting impatient for his call."

"You can't call me that." Cooper started cracking up. "He'll think we're nuts or that we have some kind of superhero fetish too."

I tried to picture Jackson trying to research that too and

figuring out how it would all work together. "Probably not a good idea."

Cooper had worked so late that by the time we'd eaten and he'd gotten a shower, it was almost time to call Jackson. We teased and talked about regular stuff, trying not to appear nervous, but as the time got closer, we both grew quieter.

When Cooper washed down the table for the second time and started pacing around the room, I knew we couldn't put it off any longer. We were only a few minutes early, but the way Cooper's nerves were starting to rattle, he was going to explode if we waited.

"Come on, he's probably ready for us to call."

Cooper stopped and looked over at me, then down at the phone on the table. "You don't think we should wait a few more minutes?"

"I think if five minutes makes a difference to him, then he's not someone we want to get to know anyway."

Shrugging, Cooper started slowly walking to the couch. I'd been pretending to play with my phone for the last few minutes, so it was easy to scoot over and make room for him. When he was sitting right next to me, I picked up the phone and brought up the email.

Copying the phone number, it only took seconds to start the phone ringing. Hitting the speaker button, I didn't protest when Cooper grabbed my free hand and hung on for dear life. I looked outwardly calmer, but inside, I wasn't much better than he was.

When the call connected, I could hear Cooper hold his breath.

"Hello?" The voice was rich and deep. It was easy to picture Jackson keeping biological dogs, or us as pups, under control without having to yell at all. It took us both a second to realize we needed to respond.

Cooper either recovered first or his brain totally

malfunctioned, and he blurted out the first thing that came to mind.

"It's Cooper and Sawyer." The words tumbled out excitedly.

Jackson chuckled. "I'm assuming this is Cooper?"

"Great." I sighed, hopefully too low for Jackson to hear.

Cooper was going into full-blown hyperactive puppy mode. "Yes, and Sawyer is here too. Sawyer, say hi."

Whispering low, I bumped his shoulder. "I'm not a kid." Then, louder, I tried to sound reasonable. "Hi, nice to talk to you."

Jackson chuckled again. *Great. He heard us.* "It's nice to talk to you too."

I'd had nothing but questions running through my mind since we'd read the email, but suddenly my brain was blank. Luckily, Cooper didn't have that problem. "Dinner sounds like fun. How was your work today? What kind of classes did you teach? What are your classes like?"

The questions came tumbling out, and I wasn't sure Jackson would be able to follow them. There was the sound of movement from his side of the phone, and I pictured him curled up on his couch. When he started speaking again, there was still a smile in his voice, but he didn't seem to mind Cooper's excitement.

"I have a lot of younger, less experienced groups in my classes right now and a handful of more advanced training sessions. Tonight was mostly puppies. And they're excitable groups." Jackson laughed, and I was picturing him leaning back on the couch remembering his classes. "They're a handful, but you can't help but enjoy it when you see them running everywhere and exploring. It's mostly about socializing the little ones and getting them used to being around strange people and new dogs." It was clear from the sound of his voice that Jackson loved his job.

I was still trying to make the connection between my mouth

and my brain work, so I wasn't sure what to say. However, I thought the easiest response would be about his work, but Cooper's brain took the conversation in a different direction.

"You sound like you love your job and watching the puppies. Do you think you'd have as much fun watching pups like us?"

God bless my excitable Coop.

Jackson was quiet for a moment, and it was the longest five seconds of my life. I couldn't tell if he was shocked or just surprised by Cooper's question, but it made my stomach whirl. Cooper didn't seem to have the same issues; he watched the phone like the silence was nothing significant.

Finally, Jackson cleared his throat. "I think it would depend on how I felt about the pups. I think as long as there is a connection between myself and the pups, feelings, I would enjoy watching them." There was another pause, but that time I was too relieved to even come up with an emotional response.

He wasn't completely freaked and could actually say that out loud. I was going to count it as a point in our favor. When Jackson started to speak again, his voice was deeper and sounded smoother, but I wasn't sure if that was because it was what I wanted to hear. "It's not a lifestyle that I would have ever considered for me personally. But the more research I do, and the more I read about it, I'm finding that it's something I can relate to."

Wow.

Cooper couldn't resist. His mind went right to the gutter, teasing and flirting. "What kind of research have you been doing?"

That sexy voice, with just a touch of naughtiness was so him, but I wasn't sure how Jackson would take it. I probably shouldn't have worried. "Sawyer, does he really look that innocent in person? In the picture, he seems like he'd be too sweet to say something like that."

I laughed, and Cooper gave me a wicked grin. "He's worse. If we're not careful, he looks like a kid I'm babysitting, and we get crazy responses because he doesn't act like people are expecting. We actually had to leave a bar one time because they thought his ID was just a really good fake."

Jackson chuckled. "So he's that naughty all the time?"

Cooper was grinning ear to ear again and nodding so enthusiastically I thought he'd give himself whiplash. But thankfully, he kept his mouth shut that time. "Yes, he's um…" Might as well be honest. "Egging people on to get a spanking is a pastime he thoroughly enjoys."

Another long pause. "Interesting."

That was it?

No, thank God. "Sometimes pups do need discipline." Hearing him say that was so hot we both almost melted into the couch. "But Cooper likes being a naughty puppy?"

Cooper sighed. "God, yes."

Jackson laughed—a rich, deep sound that sent shivers through both of us. "I don't have a problem with that at all. But is there anything more specific BDSM-wise that you're looking for in a…partner?"

Not exactly sure what he was asking, I tried to guess. "No, we're not into anything hard-core, just the puppy play…um… spankings…maybe being restrained a little. That's it."

Dating had gone all kinds of weird when someone could honestly say "that's it" to spankings and being restrained.

"Okay. I'm comfortable with those limits." There seemed to be a bit of relief in his voice. How weird had his research gotten?

"And we *are* looking for a partner. A third." Cooper's excitement was starting to boil over again. "We want something serious. We don't want to jump right in and do anything stupid, but we're looking for someone who would be a long-term member of our family."

It was nice that Cooper had been paying attention, but I wasn't sure Jackson needed to hear that I'd told him we weren't going to do anything stupid. Jackson seemed to appreciate what he was saying, though. "I can understand that. I spoke with someone who's familiar with the lifestyle, and she said that it created a stronger bond between people faster than I would expect."

"Who?"

"Who?"

Jackson chuckled. "My sister evidently writes dirty romance novels. I'm not sure exactly what kind, but she's the one who got the ad mixed up. It was surprising, but she's actually had a lot of interesting things to say about the lifestyle."

"Does she know there's two of us?" Cooper leaned toward the phone, eyes wide, biting his lip.

Jackson's voice was cautious. "Yes. Is that okay? I didn't think it was something I needed to hide from her."

Cooper's wide eyes turned to me, and he mouthed the words excitedly. *He told his sister about us!* Then he responded to Jackson. "That's fine. We don't want to hide anything."

I was just as excited, but what did it mean?

"Good." Jackson's voice evened out, and I thought it sounded like he was relieved to hear Cooper's answer. "Although, I don't think people need to know everything."

Cooper giggled; there was no other way to describe the sound. "Yes. They don't need to know we're pups."

"I would have to agree with that. But I know that a lot of pups and their masters attend different groups and meetings. Have you gone to any?"

"No." Cooper shook his head like Jackson could actually see him, and I had to fight not to smile. "We decided that seemed a little overwhelming, especially since we're both pups. We've talked to people online, though."

"That makes sense. There's a lot about all of this that's a

little overwhelming, but I'd like to get to know you better and learn more about what you're looking for. Does dinner still sound like a good idea, or do you need time to talk it over?"

Cooper managed to restrain himself enough to look over at me, which I appreciated. I shrugged and pointed to him. I was good with it as long as he was. He started nodding again and beamed at the phone. "Dinner sounds great. What time?"

As they talked about schedules and flirted, I couldn't help but stare at the phone in shock. I'd never actually thought we'd meet someone who would be open to getting to know us both. It felt a little surreal.

Cooper was so sweet and lovable; I knew someone could easily fall for him, but Jackson honestly seemed excited to talk to Cooper *and* me. I hoped that as we kept whatever it was we were doing going, he was still just as interested in both of us.

Jackson seemed like the kind of guy that would fit right in with our family. He seemed to balance out Cooper's excitement, and that warm, deep voice made me want to curl into it.

I hoped he was the same person when we met him. Cooper didn't need any more disappointments.

9

COOPER

"Are you ready?" I tried to sound cheerful, but it was getting harder.

"Not anymore ready than the last three times you asked, Coop."

I'd waited five minutes between the last two times, so I didn't think it was that bad. Sawyer, however, did not seem to be impressed. But if he'd hurried, I wouldn't have needed to ask again. He'd been primping and dawdling in the bathroom for over twenty minutes.

He was normally a five-minutes-and-he's-out kind of guy. Even when he was really focused on how he looked, he never took more than ten.

He was driving me crazy.

Flopping back onto the bed, I stared up at the ceiling. "He's going to think you look sexy. Stop obsessing."

There was a short pause that felt very long. "I'm not obsessing."

Rather than get into a "yes you are, no I'm not" discussion, I rolled my eyes, whispering, "Of course you're not."

Sawyer was sexy and had this serious brooding look that

made you want to kiss him or do something to him to make him smile. I'd never seen him this worked up over anything. Not that I'd seen him go on that many dates. Well, none really.

So maybe the primping was normal for him?

Probably not.

I couldn't imagine high school Sawyer taking this long to get ready for anything, much less what was probably a quickie with someone random. And we'd been talking about finding a master for a while, but we'd never gotten this close to meeting anyone.

Most of the time, we got the creeps because they came across as weird, or they backed out because we weren't what they were expecting. So maybe I was starting to get the picture. Was Sawyer worried that Jackson wouldn't like us...wouldn't like how he looked?

I thought our differences only made us look hotter together. And Jackson seemed like the kind of guy that would see it too. He'd understood right away that we were individuals and that it wasn't a one-size-fits-all kind of relationship. To me, it seemed like he'd gone out of his way to show us he understood that.

Why wouldn't it be the same when it came to how we looked?

After the first phone call, he'd spent the rest of the night and most of Friday texting us. With me, he ended up flirting and teasing, mostly. With Sawyer, they seemed to talk about work and more regular stuff. But with a little encouragement, I got them both to have a bit more fun with their texts.

Jackson hadn't taken much pushing at all.

A simple flirty comment about how he should tell Sawyer what he thought of his picture and Jackson had picked up the challenge. Of course, he'd told on me too, but the way Sawyer blushed and struggled to text back was worth it.

I'd never pictured Sawyer as submissive when we were in high school. Nothing in his "tops and bottoms" lecture made wanting to bottom sound like the same things I was feeling. It was one of the reasons I hadn't told him about the puppy-play stuff and how watching it made me feel. He seemed so strong and steady to me that I thought there was no way he'd understand.

I couldn't have been more wrong.

He understood the submission part completely. I think it was something he'd just started exploring himself, so maybe the timing was right, but the puppy-play part took a little longer. But he'd watched videos with me and read articles, anything he could to understand what I liked and what was drawing me to it.

By the time we could afford some toys and things to actually see how it would feel, we were a family, and he was curious, so it all worked out. But we were never going to move forward with everything if he didn't get out of the bathroom.

"Sawyer?"

"Yes?" His voice came from a lot closer than I was expecting. Sitting up, I grinned. He was finally done.

"You look hot." He really did.

Jackson said one of his favorite places to eat was a diner that we'd passed by but had never gone in, so we were both casually dressed. That didn't mean we hadn't worried about how we'd look. I was grateful he hadn't picked somewhere too fancy. The idea of something like that would've been overwhelming, and most of our clothes would have been too casual.

Sawyer's dark jeans were molded to his legs, though they couldn't be called skinny jeans. He'd worked outside for so long that he was too muscular and well-defined. His dark hair was just long enough that I could run my fingers through it. Tonight, he'd clearly worked to tame it, so there was no way he was going to let me play with it.

The shirt he was wearing outlined his broad chest and would have been a little too tight for work, but for our date, he looked perfect. "If you'd gotten ready sooner, we'd have time for some fun before we left."

He smirked, but there were still shadows in his eyes. "Stress relief?"

"Yup." I let my eyes close halfway, and I stretched back against the bed. My jeans were even tighter, but they emphasized how lean I was, and as Sawyer said, what a great ass I had. If I stretched just right, they drew attention to my cock when it was hard. I was normally very well-behaved in public, but sometimes teasing Sawyer was fun.

He groaned. "No distracting me."

"But—"

He shook his head, but his eyes were still wandering over my chest and down to my cock. "No buts. We've got to go. I don't want to be late."

I gave him an innocent look I knew was perfect and blinked up at him. "I'll tell him why we were late, though. He'd understand."

Sawyer licked his lips, and I could see his imagination flaring to life, but I had a feeling I wasn't the only one he was picturing in bed at that moment. He was a little cagey about admitting he was starting to like Jackson, but I knew him too well to miss the fantasies running through his head.

Sawyer took his time making a decision. He'd planned out how he was going to leave home for years. He'd researched different careers, figured out how he could make things work, and had obsessively looked over our budget before we'd gotten our first car.

He'd even gone through everything in his head over and over before he accepted that he wasn't just a bottom but was submissive as well. I wasn't expecting dating or finding a master to be any different, but that didn't make it any easier to watch.

Once we met Jackson, and Sawyer saw that he was as nice in person as he'd been on the phone, everything would get easier. Sawyer probably thought I was a little naïve about it all, but that wasn't it. Jackson just felt right, and Sawyer was afraid to admit it.

Finally, his grown-up side made the decision for him, unfortunately. "We don't want to make him wait. He already texted a few minutes ago that he was on his way."

Spoilsport.

I'd been horny most of the day, but work and some unplanned overtime kept me from being able to do anything about it. Sawyer needed some time to turn everything off. This was all more stressful for him than he was willing to admit.

I tried to remember the last time he'd been a pup and cuddled up to me. But it had been so long, I couldn't think of it. Bringing it up before the date would probably give him too much to think about, but I made a mental note to make sure he got to play when we got home.

He was usually so convincing about letting me play and telling me he wanted to stay out of his role, so he could throw the ball, that I didn't even think about it. The times that I had started to protest, he kept telling me that he'd be the pup next time.

I was going to have to learn to stand my ground better, so he didn't always have to be the one still thinking. It was too easy to let him make the decisions about stuff like that. But it wasn't really fair to him. I needed to remember that he needed playtime and submission as much as I did.

He just never came out and said it.

Sighing dramatically, Sawyer rolled his eyes. I got out of bed and struck a pose. "He's going to think I'm sexy, won't he?"

Sawyer laughed. "Of course he will. Come on, goof."

Heading out of the room, I might have gotten a little excited, but we were finally going to meet Jackson, so I couldn't help it.

"Coop, you're going to make me dizzy if you keep dancing

around like that. He'll think we're nuts." Sawyer sighed again, but I could hear it was just the stress.

"Ha, if me flirting on the phone didn't scare him off, my excitement won't scare him either."

"What did you text him on the phone?" Sawyer sounded half-worried and half like he was trying to ignore how perfect I was.

I gave him a big grin as we walked out the door. "All kinds of things."

"Oh, Coop."

"Don't 'oh, Coop' me. He asked what kinds of things I was interested in, so I told him."

Sawyer gave me a long look as we headed down the stairs. "Coooop…" He drew out the word, trying to sound all in charge. He was just jealous he hadn't worked up the nerve to be as interestingly honest yet. "Is that really what he asked?"

I giggled; there was no way to even call it a laugh. "Basically."

Jackson *might* have meant what kinds of hobbies I had, but he hadn't really been specific. When people were texting, it needed to be clear what they meant. Jackson was learning that quickly, and it was so much fun to teach him.

I was definitely going to be spanked before Sawyer.

Sawyer was still shaking his head, mumbling about Jackson thinking we were crazy when we got to the car. Dinner was going to be fun.

"WE LOOK FINE. HE'S GOING TO THINK WE'RE FABULOUS. And he's here already. So getting out of the car is a must." Sawyer looked a little like he was going to throw up, and I wasn't sure my pep talk helped. I might have needed more practice.

But it really wasn't meant to, though. He was the type of person who needed to see that it would work out. In his head, he was a little pessimistic. But that was what he had me for. Grabbing his hand, I leaned over the console between us and gave him a kiss. "At the very least, we get a funny story to tell our perfect master when he finally falls into our life and a good free dinner. Come on."

"Free dinner and a funny story, huh? Who could resist that?" Sawyer began to relax, and I got a little smile from him as he started to climb out of the car.

As I shut the car door, I nodded. "Yup. The reviews on this place are better than you'd think."

He started walking around the car, looking at me like I was nuts. "You looked it up?"

When Jackson had mentioned that he liked the restaurant, I'd been curious. At first glance, with its gravel parking lot and slightly rough looking exterior, it hadn't seemed that impressive. I'd even done the whole street-view thing to look around the neighborhood, but nothing struck me as that special, so I'd looked them up on every site I could think of. I'd wanted to know why it was Jackson's favorite restaurant.

"Of course. I'm getting the pancakes." *Duh.*

"For dinner?" He cocked his head and glanced over at the front of the restaurant. He really should have done some research.

"You obviously didn't read the reviews, or you wouldn't have even asked me that question." Taking his hand, I started hurrying him toward the building. I was excited to meet Jackson in person, and I was starving. "And how am I supposed to know why he likes it if I don't look it up?"

"You could try actually talking to him and not just flirting." Sawyer's tone was dry, but his eyes sparkled as he reached for the door handle.

"That wouldn't be as much fun, though." A deep voice came from behind us, and I turned excitedly.

"Jackson!" He was taller than I'd expected; his broad frame almost towered over me and even made Sawyer seem small at first glance.

He looked just like his pictures.

Even Sawyer must have liked what he saw. His grip relaxed in mine, and I could feel the stress easing out of him. Sawyer gave him a warm smile but shook his head. "You shouldn't encourage him."

I blinked up at Jackson, and then looked at Sawyer, a little pout on my face. "But even you said I'm incorrigible, so that means he should encourage me."

"Don't believe that dumb blond act for a minute. He got As in everything and just about aced the SAT."

"Tattletale." I'd already told Jackson about college and my goals, so I wasn't trying to look dumb, but making him smile was fun.

"There's a comment here about what happens to naughty boys who fight, but I'm going to behave, so I won't say anything like that." Jackson grinned as Sawyer blushed, then he turned to me and winked.

I loved that he wasn't afraid to flirt with me but still tried to make Sawyer feel special without being overwhelmed. Sawyer thought we'd just been flirting and teasing, but I'd spent a little while grilling Jackson on what he thought about Sawyer.

He was good about not sharing secrets—not that Sawyer and I had any—but he told me enough to make me think that they were really clicking, even if Sawyer was dragging his feet. But I knew Sawyer would come around in time. And I also knew, from what Jackson had said and what he hadn't, that he wasn't going to rush either of us beyond what we were comfortable with.

He was going to be the perfect master.

He let me flirt and tease, but his comment let us both know that he wasn't going to shy away from punishments. I could only imagine how he would be when I was a pup. He'd be fun and indulgent as I played but would ground me and make me feel safe.

I just knew it.

I also knew we had to go into the restaurant at some point, or I'd never get fed. We were still standing around outside the building, and while he was technically still almost a stranger, it didn't feel that way. Sawyer let go of my hand and reached to shake Jackson's.

That was fine for him, but I was getting more than a handshake. How would I know if there was chemistry without a little bit of contact? As they parted, I threw myself at Jackson, wrapping my arms around him in a hug.

I behaved myself: quick hug and let go and no groping him or getting too close. But the feel of his muscled back and the strength of his arms as they wrapped around me was giving me second thoughts on it.

"I'm starving." I gave him a grin and was relieved when I saw the warmth in his eyes. "You need to feed me."

"Of course, and they have the best—"

"Pancakes! I saw the reviews online. I want ones with bananas and chocolate chips." I'd been planning dinner for hours.

Jackson laughed and reached out to run his fingers through my hair. It was an almost unconscious gesture, and it made my toes curl because it was so easy to imagine the same gentle touch when I was a pup. I was smart enough not to ask, though.

And Sawyer thought I had no common sense.

"You both sound crazy." Sawyer was looking at us like we'd lost our minds.

Jackson didn't seem to mind. He started to explain my excitement, so he was also feeling more generous than I was.

"They make the best pancakes. They make them to order and have something like fifty mix-ins and toppings you can choose. And they're—"

"Huge!"

"How much coffee did you have at work today?"

Oops.

"I don't know exactly." I'd been so excited, and employee drinks were free, and thinking back, I wasn't sure how many I'd gotten.

The chocolate one.

The white chocolate one.

The new one that had the sprinkles on top.

And there were at least a few more thrown in there.

Oops.

Jackson was laughing so hard people across the parking lot turned to stare. I shrugged, and Sawyer rolled his eyes. "It was *too* much."

Finally catching his breath, Jackson reached out to squeeze Sawyer's shoulder and then gave me a smile. "No more caffeine for you. And how about we get some food in you?"

Sawyer chuckled. "I think that's just for soaking up alcohol, but at the very least, it will keep his mouth busy."

There were so many naughty things I could have said to that.

Evidently Jackson thought of them too, because he coughed a bit and gave Sawyer a look. It took Sawyer a minute to realize what he'd said, and then he blushed again, grumbling about men with dirty minds. Since he loved mine, though, I wasn't worried about it. Jackson didn't seem to take it personally either, but he did ruffle my hair and point to the door.

"Are we ready for dinner? I think someone's starving."

Sawyer nodded gratefully, seemingly appreciating the change of subject. "Yes. I can't wait to see what else they have."

"Sawyer thinks that breakfast should stay at breakfast."

Jackson sucked in a breath dramatically, laughter shining in his eyes. "That's sacrilegious. This is holy breakfast ground."

"I know! I saw it in the reviews." Sawyer groaned and reached for the door, clearly giving up on making us behave. "We're going to have to convert him."

Jackson nodded. "Or we could do this together sometimes, and I could find somewhere that Sawyer would appreciate to take him? From what I've read, it's important that people in a relationship like the one you're looking for make the time to have strong bonds as couples, not just as a group."

Then he seemed to realize how long-term that sounded because he kept going. "Not that I'm assuming anything. This is a first date, and you might decide that we don't fit right together."

He was trying to be serious, and I tried not to grin, but it sounded dirty. Sawyer looked at me, shaking his head. I was doing my best, though, so I nodded. "I'm starting to think another date sounds like a good idea. So we can get to know each other better."

As I walked in the door, Sawyer leaned close and whispered. "Little tease."

"I'm not a tease, and you'll find that out when we get home." Then I winked at him and tried to look innocent as Jackson grinned and attempted to pretend he hadn't heard us.

Sawyer was still shaking his head as the hostess came up. I might have been driving him just a little bit crazy, but he was relaxed and no longer looked like he was going to vomit, so I was counting the date as a win.

Pancakes, a sexy learning-to-be-almost-Dom, and Sawyer by my side…yup…perfect date.

Okay, so aside from Sawyer, it was probably my only date. But still…perfect.

10

JACKSON

The evening couldn't have gone better, even with Sawyer ordering a hamburger. Cooper was still slightly miffed that Sawyer wouldn't pick out pancakes like we had. The entire time, he grumbled about Sawyer loving pancakes with blueberries and strawberries in them.

Even as Cooper had stuffed the last of his dinner-plate-sized pancakes into his mouth—he was a bottomless pit—he was still mumbling that Sawyer was going to regret the decision in the morning. If I was honest, I was going to have to say that Cooper was right because Sawyer was giving the pancakes some long looks.

But finally, Sawyer looked over at me and grinned. "And this is why he needs a spanking on a regular basis. I'm going to hear about the stupid pancakes for days."

Cooper nodded, clearly enthusiastic about the plan. As soon as he swallowed, though, he threw Sawyer under the bus too. "And that snarky comment is why *he* needs a spanking on a regular basis too. He's much more relaxed after. And being a pup more—"

Sawyer shoved a fry into Cooper's mouth.

I tried not to laugh and ended up coughing into my napkin like I was choking. I couldn't decide if Cooper said stuff without thinking, or if he loved getting a reaction, but I was leaning toward the latter.

His I'm-so-innocent smile was just too perfect most of the time.

"One day he's just going to throw something at you." I was expecting them to laugh, but Sawyer blushed a wonderful purple color and Cooper started to nod.

What the hell had they done?

"He threw his tail at me. Do you know how hard it is to explain away a bruise that looks like a dick?" Cooper was so earnest and matter-of-fact, I was shocked.

I started coughing and couldn't catch my breath. They were the funniest people I'd ever met. Sawyer was trying so hard to be calm and not let anyone see how nervous he was, and Cooper was bouncy and open and honest to a fault most of the time.

Especially when it would drive Sawyer crazy.

"Why did you throw your tail at him?" I was very proud of myself for not stumbling over that question.

Sawyer's coloring hadn't gone back to normal, and his head fell back, so he was staring up at the ceiling. "I wasn't trying to throw it at him. He was going on and on about something, and I was frustrated and started talking with my hands, and the damn thing went flying."

Then his head came up, and he stared at Cooper, his voice dropping low. "And stop saying it looked like a dick. It did not."

Cooper snorted. "It did too. It looked like your cock slapped into my thigh so hard it left a bruise."

Lord, they were a handful.

But so perfect, I couldn't help wanting to gather them in my arms. Cooper seemed to be craving a firm hand to help him settle down. Sawyer was a little harder to read, but all I wanted to do was hold him and tell him it was okay to let himself surrender.

So I thought that was a pretty good guess about what he needed.

Sawyer rolled his eyes and almost had his blush under control when Cooper struck again. He gave me that innocently sweet look, and I knew it was going to be good, or terrible, depending on his mood. "The bruise was too small to be his dick, though."

Was he saying...? My brain had a hard time formulating a response.

"Cooper." Sawyer's voice was low but harsh. He couldn't seem to decide if he wanted to laugh or let his head fall to the table in exasperation.

"Well, it's true. You're much bigger than that bruise."

Yup, that was what he'd meant.

Luckily, our waitress took that moment to stop back by the table, giving Sawyer a chance to recover. "Jackson, you guys want any dessert?" One eyebrow went up. "Not sure either of you two needs any more sugar, though."

Sawyer laughed. "No, they don't."

Cooper looked over at him, wide eyes giving Sawyer a pleading look. "But they have—"

I could see Sawyer weakening, and I took a chance. I was hoping he wouldn't get upset with me. "No." Then I turned to the waitress, who I'd met several times before. "Jennifer, we're fine. I think he's had enough sugar for one day."

She said something about coming to check on us again in a minute, but my focus was completely on Sawyer. Cooper craved someone to take control, but I wasn't sure how Sawyer would react. He took a breath and turned to look at me. Caution was clear on his face, but there was also a relief that I couldn't define.

I'd been doing as much research as I could, trying to

understand what they were looking for. But no amount of reading or videos could really let me comprehend how it would feel to know something was missing in your life or to know that as much as they loved each other, he couldn't be everything for Cooper.

It was easy to see that he tried.

I hadn't pieced together much of the story about how they'd become a family, but I was used to reading people and their dogs. Sawyer's entire focus was on Cooper, and it was clear he'd do anything for him.

Friend.

Lover.

Family.

However they defined their relationship, I could see it was unbreakable.

Maybe that should have scared me. Maybe I should have been worried about possibly joining a couple who was so tightly bonded together, but it sent relief flooding through me. They were solid. They loved each other more than any other couple I'd ever met. They'd each pushed aside their own needs and desires to focus on the other, and that wasn't something I saw in most relationships.

Watching them, I knew that nothing I did, no inadvertent screw-up or misplaced words, would tear them apart. And I also knew that this was something that they'd thought out and discussed. A couple that close, one who knew each other as well as they did, wouldn't do anything like this unless they knew without a doubt that it was what the other person desperately wanted.

What they both desperately wanted.

Sawyer was quiet, but either he was starting to let his guard down, or I was getting better at reading him, because I could see a warmth to him and something seemed to have settled in him. We were taking it slow, and I knew we weren't at a point where I could ask, but everything in me wanted to know what was going through his mind.

Cooper broke the silence by sighing. And we both looked over to see his elbows on the table, and his face cradled in his hands. "All you two need is a bowl of spaghetti. It's just so cute I want popcorn."

I was lost.

Sawyer took pity on me. "*Lady and the Tramp*. He's seen it like a thousand times."

"Ohhh." It had been years since I'd seen the movie, but it came flooding back, and I gave Cooper a long look with one eyebrow raised. "If I'm remembering that movie correctly, I'm neither Lady nor the Tramp."

Cooper giggled. Sawyer shook his head and turned to give me a teasing look. "He's definitely Lady. I'll be the Tramp, and you can be our new master."

It wasn't a complete invitation into their life, but I knew it was his way of letting me know that he felt the same connection I did. I wasn't sure where it was going or how everything would end up working out, but I couldn't wait to find out.

Cooper missed the exchange, still focusing on the movie. He snorted and gave us both a look like we were crazy. "Disney does not make those kinds of movies." Then he grinned. "And of course I get to be Lady."

When his face turned serious, I thought something was wrong—nope, just Cooper being Cooper. "But only if I get a bigger tail. Hers was too short."

I was left speechless again.

I glanced at Sawyer, and he shrugged like it was nothing. Finally, he started to explain. "It was one of those movies that he loved as a kid, but once you get to be a certain age, people think it's weird if you still like it, so when he—when we started living together, and he finally told me about the puppy-play stuff, it was the first present I bought for him."

Cooper was grinning ear to ear. "What he's leaving out is that he could only find a VHS tape of the movie and had to go to three thrift stores to find a VCR that would play it. And this was before we got a car, so he had to take buses all over town just to surprise me with it."

I was missing pieces of their past, but it was easy to tell that things had been hard for them. That Sawyer had gone to so much trouble to make Cooper happy made me even more sure I'd read them right. "I bet you wore out that tape."

Sawyer laughed. "He's starting to know you."

Cooper nodded. "And now it's on my computer and on DVD, so I don't have to chase down a VCR to play it."

"I didn't even think those were still around."

Shrugging, Cooper nodded again. "They seem to be the cockroaches of the machine world. When everything else is dead and unresponsive, there will be stacks of VCRs in old junk shops that still work."

Laughing, I had to agree. "Aliens will come to our planet long after we're gone and all they'll find is VCRs and bugs."

"Don't egg him on." Sawyer was leaning back in his chair and smiling.

"But he's so much fun to play with." Giving Cooper a long look, I continued. "And I think no matter how he wants to play, he'll be just as much fun."

I wasn't sure if they would understand what I was trying to say, but Cooper grinned and wiggled in his seat a little, and Sawyer's posture relaxed more, and he sank into the chair, making me realize how stiffly he'd been holding himself.

He wasn't the bouncy type that showed his happiness and emotions the same way that Cooper did, but when people took the time to get to know him and to really look, I thought it would be as obvious as Cooper's wagging tail—which was an image I couldn't help but try to picture.

Cooper leaned closer and dropped his voice. "I like balls."

I was hoping he was talking about toys—only because we were in public, though.

"I saw a lot of pups online that had toys and liked to play with them." Cooper had vaguely mentioned that most of the time they took turns being pups, so I wasn't sure exactly how they worked it out, but I was going to go out on a limb. "Does Sawyer throw the ball for you?"

Nodding, Cooper didn't seem embarrassed by the turn the conversation had taken. "Yes, but our apartment doesn't have a lot of space to run."

I had the perfect space for a pup to run. Had he seen the pictures online? They'd both mentioned that they'd seen the photos of me online, but they hadn't talked about the facilities. It was probably too soon to bring it up, but it was a nagging image in my head that wouldn't go away.

Deciding to push my luck again, I leaned closer to Cooper and gave Sawyer a look. "Does Sawyer like to play ball?"

Sawyer took an immediate fascination with his silverware but didn't tell either of us to back off, so I glanced back at Cooper. He shook his head. "No, he's more of a cuddly pup. He's like one of those big dogs who don't understand they aren't lap dogs anymore and still wants to curl up with you on the couch."

"I bet he'd be great to cuddle with."

Cooper smiled and glanced at Sawyer who was starting to inspect his fork. "He is. He's definitely an apartment kind of dog."

"But you're a pup who'd like some space?"

Again, he answered without fear. His wide smile lit up his face. "Yes."

What was the old expression? In for a penny, in for a pound? "I'd like to see you like that someday when we're all ready. I'd like to play with you and get to know that side of you."

Cooper finally blushed, but it didn't diminish his ear-to-ear grin as he glanced over at Sawyer before nodding. "When we're all ready."

"There's no rush. I'm not going anywhere." I had a feeling *that* was going to end up being an understatement.

We talked and teased for a few more minutes, but eventually, Jennifer brought the check by, and it was lying there like a beacon that screamed out our date was over. Part of me wanted to see if they'd like to go to a movie or something, but I knew they needed a chance to talk things out before we took it any further.

Knowing they were going to head home together, and I was going to be alone, was weird. Not bad, but odd.

They waited with me while I paid. Signing the receipt, I turned to smile at them. "I had a wonderful time. Thank you for agreeing to come with me to dinner."

"We have to come back for more pancakes." Cooper glanced over at the table, longingly.

"Of course. Maybe next time, you can try the chocolate strawberry ones you were thinking about."

Cooper nodded. "And you can pick Sawyer's brain for a place that you two can go while I work late some night."

Turning to Sawyer, I stepped toward the door, so we could get out of the way. "If you like burgers, I know a great place."

He smiled and nodded. "That sounds good." There was a little pause before Sawyer glanced at Cooper. "You work late next Thursday, don't you?"

Cooper discreetly took my hand and gave it a quick squeeze as we started piling out the door. "Yes, it's a late night to begin with, and my manager wants to show me some inventory procedures, so it's going to be even later than usual."

Taking Cooper's hint, I looked at Sawyer. "Would you like to go try it out then? I have classes until seven that night, but after that, I'm free."

Turning a little pink, Sawyer nodded hesitantly. "It sounds like fun."

"Great." Cooper started almost bouncing through the parking lot. "And pancakes with me on Saturday morning? I don't have to work until ten."

"It's a date then." As we got closer to their car, I was regretting not making the date longer. Asking them out to dinner had seemed a bit like we were rushing things, but I'd clearly underestimated how much fun we'd have. "Two dates, really."

Sawyer paused by their car, leaning up against the black compact trying to look casual but failing. "And you're okay with that?"

"The separate dates, or the dates in general?"

"Um, both probably. I don't want us to rush you." His words came out carefully, but I wasn't sure if he was trying to give me an out or if he was getting overwhelmed.

"I had a lot of fun with you both tonight and want to do it again. But I also like the idea of getting to know you separately. To really see if we're going to work, I think doing things together and as couples would be important." They were both very different people, and I wanted to make sure I knew who Sawyer was without Cooper egging him on, and Cooper when there wasn't anything else to focus on but us.

Sawyer's head bobbed up and down, and his body seemed to relax again. I wasn't sure how well I was reading him, but he seemed to be the worrier of their family, and I was having the damnedest time holding myself back. I wasn't sure he was ready to let me step in and be the person he could share those fears with.

"Is this a kiss-at-the-end date or just a hug and see you next week kind?" Cooper's expression was so open and honest, I had to smile.

Sawyer started to chuckle, but he looked relieved that he

THE ACCIDENTAL MASTER

didn't have to figure it out for himself. Cooper was one corner of our triangle as we stood by the car, but he didn't even blink as I took a step closer. "What were you imagining, Pup? Judging by that grin and that sexy blush, if I had to guess, I'd say you wanted a kiss."

Cooper started rocking back and forth on his heels, nodding excitedly. "Yes. A perfect first date like this needs a knock-your-socks-off kiss at the end."

"Knock your socks off, huh?" But before I could decide how he would define that, Sawyer spoke up unexpectedly.

"Hey, I was more well-behaved at dinner than you were. I think I get the first kiss." He was clearly nervous, but I wasn't going to call him out on that. Whatever he was doing, I knew he had his reasons.

"He's right, Pup. He didn't try to get dessert, and he didn't tell funny stories just to make you blush." Cooper was grinning. Evidently he didn't mind Sawyer getting a kiss as long as he got to watch.

"Yes, kisses." He waved a hand back and forth. "I don't get to see him when we kiss and stuff because he won't let me record it."

Sawyer laughed. "No home movies."

"Spoilsport. But now I get to see." I thought it was funny that he was more excited about Sawyer getting a kiss than he was about getting his own.

Reaching out, I took Sawyer's hand in mine. It was shaking a little, but his face didn't give me any indication I should take a step back and put a stop to our first kiss. Not wanting to trap him between my body and the car, I pulled him close and turned so that I was the one leaning against the hood.

He fit against me perfectly.

He wasn't quite as tall as me, but he was broad and felt substantial in my arms like he belonged there. Bringing my free hand up to his face, I let my fingers caress the side of his cheek

107

and trace the hairs that were curling around his ears. His short hair was more businesslike than Cooper's, but it was just as touchable.

Sawyer sighed and leaned into my hand, closing his eyes. It wasn't complete submission, but I knew it was the first step. His body was screaming out for what he desperately wanted. Bringing my mouth down to his, I kept the first touch of our lips light, just the barest pressure while they moved against each other.

If we didn't have our sexy audience sighing and cooing over how cute we were, I would have probably ended it there, but with Cooper watching, I wanted to let him see how beautiful Sawyer was. Moving away from his lips, I kissed up his jaw while he moaned, the little shivers racing through him getting stronger.

When I finally got to his ear, I teased the sensitive skin with my tongue, loving the way he was coming apart in my hands. Between kisses, I whispered low, just for him, "I'll never rush you. But I'll be here when you're ready to let me in."

As I pulled back, frustrated that I had to let him go, he opened his eyes and leaned in for a hug. As his arms wrapped around me, I heard a quiet, "Thank you." Before he pulled back, I heard more words that I knew were just for me. "He's never really had a first-date kiss."

Giving him a kiss on the cheek, I stepped away. He'd do anything for Cooper, even putting himself out there when he wasn't sure about the outcome.

Turning to Cooper, I gave him a heated look. Cooper didn't want careful or gentle. He wanted a smoking hot kiss he would remember forever. And I was going to do my best to give it to him. "Did you like watching Sawyer get kissed?"

Nothing was going to stop me from letting them both know they were sexy, and I loved our first date. However, I was glad that we didn't have an audience in the parking lot. Cooper's eyes were wide and filled with need, and though his wiggling hadn't really stopped, it looked more about desire than sheer excitement.

"You're both so hot! It was perfect." So cute and open.

Reaching out, I took a step forward and grabbed his hand. When his fingers wrapped tightly around mine, I pulled him close, so he was flush against me, his body fitting into mine perfectly. Cooper gasped in surprise, but when his free hand reached out to pull me even closer, I didn't second-guess my actions.

He was so tiny I could almost wrap myself around him. Someone else might have been taken in by how young and innocent he looked, but I was starting to understand all the naughty things that went through the sexy pup's head.

Letting go of his fingers, I wrapped my hands around his waist and lifted him off the ground. I wasn't strong enough to hold him like that forever, but hearing his surprised squeak and feeling his legs wrap around me was worth it.

Sawyer was laughing, and Cooper wrapped his arms around me tightly, not even trying to hide how excited he was. Taking his mouth, I kissed him deeply, letting my tongue dance against his while he moaned and started slowly rubbing his cock against my abs. Where my kiss with Sawyer had been gentle and beautifully tender, Cooper was like holding fireworks in my arms.

When I finally pulled away, he blinked back at me, desire shining from his eyes. "You were a naughty pup in the restaurant, weren't you? Making Sawyer blush and saying outrageous things."

Cooper bit into his lower lip and gave me a contrite expression that I didn't believe for a minute. "I'll be good next time."

"We both know that's a lie, naughty pup." I gave his ass a

light tap that made him moan again. "I think you owe Sawyer a *thorough* apology later, don't you?"

Cooper's eyes widened even more, and he looked over at Sawyer hungrily. "I need to show him I'm sorry."

"That's right. You need to make it up to him, don't you?" I was going to torture myself all night with the sexy images that were running through my head, but it was worth it to see the surprised pleasure on both of their faces.

It wasn't traditional domination, but I knew they could both feel it.

"Yes, Sir. I'll be good and show him how sorry I am for being naughty." Then my sweet cutie turned and gave me a kiss on the cheek.

They were such a mix of contradictions, but it made me want to learn everything about them. Letting Cooper slide down my body, I reluctantly released him, kissing the top of his head. "I had a wonderful time with you both tonight."

Reaching out, I ran a hand over Sawyer's hair. "Dinner Thursday? I'll call you, and we'll work out the details."

He nodded, looking slightly overwhelmed by everything. "Yes. Dinner."

Letting Cooper go, I resisted the urge to kiss them one more time. No matter how difficult it was, walking away was the right move. It was just harder than it should have been. As I headed over to my car, I couldn't resist looking back one more time. Cooper's head was resting on Sawyer's shoulder, both watching me intently.

It was going to be a long night.

11

SAWYER

Cooper wrapped his arms around me and sighed. Curling up on the bed when we'd gotten home had been his idea, but it was just what I needed. Cooper had bounced off the walls the whole ride back. To him, it had been the perfect first date, and I couldn't have been happier.

When I'd whispered the words to Jackson, I wasn't sure if he'd understand. Cooper had built it up so much in his mind that a simple kiss on the cheek or peck on the lips would have been a letdown. It didn't matter that it would have been a perfectly reasonable end to a first date.

He wanted fireworks and the Dom of his dreams.

Well, he'd gotten it—we both had.

Cooper sighed dreamily, and one hand started rubbing my chest. "He spanked me."

He was like a teenage girl with her first crush...just a naughty one. "He gave your ass a swat. That wasn't a full spanking. It was a first date, slut."

Cooper giggled. "The perfect first date. Except for ours. That was perfect too."

I wasn't sure cold pizza after telling him that I loved him

counted as a first date, but Cooper always did. "At least your food was hot on this date."

Laughing, he nodded and the way his hair rubbed against my neck tickled, making me squirm. "He wants to take us both out next week. I get more pancakes."

Evidently, the way to Cooper's heart wasn't food in general, but just pancakes.

I couldn't decide how I felt. I'd kept waiting for something to go wrong. Some story that Cooper told that would show him we weren't right for him, or that he wouldn't be able to relate to us both, but everything had gone wonderfully. Even that stupid penis story.

"I can't believe you told him that butt plug story."

"Why?" I felt him shrug. "It's funny. He laughed too."

"I'm not sure that's a *first date* kind of story."

He snorted. "It might have been our first date, but he's not really a stranger. We've talked on the phone and texted tons and then there are the emails and Facebook stalking. We know him well enough to tell him the funny stuff."

"I'm not Facebook stalking him, are you?"

"Of course." His head came up, and he looked at me like I was nuts. "Why wouldn't I? He's got a business page where he posts cute pics of the dogs and stuff and his personal page where he just seems to argue with his sister. He needs to update his privacy settings—any weirdo could be watching."

For some reason, Cooper didn't understand why I thought that statement was hilarious.

By the time I stopped laughing, he was shaking his head, clearly not connecting the dots on that statement. "Come here."

Pulling him down to my chest again, I wrapped my arms around him and started caressing up and down his back. It was so easy to close my eyes and picture Jackson in bed with us, his strong body cuddled up to us. It probably should have been harder to imagine, but for some reason, he seemed to fit.

Nothing about the date had seemed forced. He honestly thought Cooper was funny and didn't mind that it took me longer to warm up. He'd made that very clear when he'd done his best to give both of us what we needed out of a goodnight kiss.

Sweet.

Tender.

Hot.

Naughty.

He'd run the gamut of what a kiss could be just because he knew Cooper's "knock my socks off" declaration wasn't something I was ready for. Not that I didn't want him. I wasn't going to pretend I didn't. He was strong and sexy and had the best laugh—rich and warm. And being out with both of us on a date didn't seem to faze him at all.

Had he honestly not noticed the odd looks?

Cooper wasn't exactly quiet either. Even the waitress had tried not to laugh several times as she'd come over to refill drinks and check on everything. Jackson's focus never wavered from us, and he didn't seem to treat us any differently than he would have treated any other date.

The feel of Cooper's lips on my neck brought my daydreams to a halt. Kissing his head, I let my hands go from soothing to arousing. When he started working his way down my body, I realized we had to be picturing two different outcomes to our evening.

"What do you want, Coop?" I tried to pull him up, but he gave me a teasing grin and shook his head.

"Master gave me instructions, and I want to be a good pup for him." Cooper then started pushing up my shirt, making it clear he was going to be *very* good.

Master's instructions, huh?

Sitting up so Cooper could take my shirt off, I lay back down and stretched out. I wasn't sure exactly what Cooper thought showing me he was sorry meant, but I was willing to find out. He always looked at everything his own way, though, so I wasn't going to try and guess.

The feel of his lips and tongue on my chest chased every thought from my head. Something about knowing he was doing it because Master told him to made it even hotter and pushed at the submissive part of me more than it usually would.

Cooper going down on me always felt incredible. Practice made perfect, and he'd wanted to be perfect for our master when we eventually found him. But being able to picture Jackson's voice as he told Cooper he needed to make it up to me put everything in a different light. Master wanted this. It wasn't about what I wanted or needed, it was about him.

So. Fucking. Hot.

Cooper must have thought so too, because I could see his hips moving as he ground his cock against the bed. Licking my abs and giving me the dirtiest looks, Cooper worked his way to my jeans and started rubbing one hand over my erection.

It wasn't enough to make me come, but imagining Jackson watching us made it even hotter. Cooper knew exactly what I was thinking, but the difference between the two of us was that he never worried about taking a fantasy to the next level. He just jumped right in.

"I can't wait to tell Master what a good pup I was and how thoroughly I apologized to you." Cooper sat up enough to unbutton my jeans and start easing the zipper down over my straining cock. "Do you think he'll reward me for being a good boy?"

The relief that flooded through me as he freed my dick made it hard to think. And his fingers wrapping around it didn't help the situation any either. "Do you want him to? Do you want him to touch you?"

God, the fantasies that were running through my head were so fuckin' sexy it was incredible. We'd teased about our fictitious master and used it as great dirty talk for so long that finally being able to put a face to the fantasy made it even better.

Cooper nodded and gave me one of those perfectly innocent smiles as he flicked his tongue out and traced around the head of my cock. *Fuck.* "I'm going to call Master and tell him that I was good, and I made you come so hard. And I'm going to ask him to tell me what kinds of rewards good pups get. What kinds of touches…" another flick of his tongue had me gasping, "… and kisses he'll give me when I'm good."

Cooper was going to set both their phones on fire.

When his lips finally closed over my dick, and he started to swallow me down, my brain gave up. The tight heat of his mouth chased every thought from my body. Cooper was a bit precocious and taught himself ridiculously young how to deep throat almost anything, so knowing what was coming made the anticipation stronger.

Hairbrush handles.

Bananas.

It would take a porn-star sized cock to make him pause and even then, it probably wouldn't stop him. He'd wanted a master since he could first jerk off. He just hadn't known what he was dreaming about until he got older.

God love the internet.

"Cooper!" His throat swallowed around the head of my cock and it sent waves of pleasure through me. Normally, I could last for ages because I'd learned stamina when he went through his "I want to be perfect for Master" phase, but in that moment, it was too much.

Meeting Jackson, his kiss, watching him push Cooper so close to the brink he'd almost come in the parking lot…it had all been too incredible.

When Cooper lifted off my dick slowly and then went back down, using his tongue to pull needy cries from my throat, I was at my breaking point. When he took me deep in his throat, and I could feel his lips on my balls, I shot.

Every muscle clenched down, and waves of pleasure flooded through me as he worked my pulsing cock. He moaned and drank me down. Cooper loved the taste of cum. I liked giving blowjobs and getting them, but I was kind of neutral on cum. Not Cooper.

When I sagged down on the bed, the last of the pleasure fading as he pulled off my dick, I expected him to curl up around me. He had something different in mind. Cooper gave me a kiss and hopped off the bed, still fully clothed and horny if his excited gestures and the bounce in his step was any clue.

"Clothes off." It was a little sing-songy, and I was confused, but I was planning on getting completely naked anyway, so I didn't see the harm.

Sometimes with Cooper, it made sense to double-check what he thought was going to happen.

But I was too tired to care.

Getting up was too much work, so I finished shoving down my pants and briefs while I lay down, only stretching to get my socks off. My body was protesting the exercise when all it wanted to do was cuddle, but it stopped arguing when I relaxed back down.

I was seriously considering how important the blanket at the end of the bed was as Cooper's head came out of the closet, a wide smile on his face. "Time for phase two."

Asking was probably stupid, but I did it anyway. "Phase two?"

Cooper shook his head like I wasn't paying attention. "I have to be able to tell Jackson that I did everything I could to make it up to you and apologize."

Everything he could?

It probably would have sounded a bit creepy if I hadn't seen my tail and collar in his hands. Then things just got jumbly in my head. There was utter relief at the idea of being able to turn everything off, but there was also a loud voice in the back of my head screaming out that Cooper was going to tell Jackson.

It was a stupid fear, because yes, we both knew Cooper would go into insane detail when he started telling Jackson about how well-behaved he'd been. And then there was the fact that Jackson already knew what we liked.

Duh, no surprise there; we'd emailed him about puppy play and masters.

But this was different. And I wasn't sure why. Did it matter that he was going to hear about a specific instance? Did it matter that Cooper was going to tell him how much I liked being a pup? Did it matter that Jackson was going to end up picturing it, trying to either understand why we did it, or possibly why he was getting off on it?

That was kind of up in the air, though, because I wasn't sure if he thought it was sexy or just interesting at that point.

Did it matter? Probably not...but it did.

But not enough to make embracing my pup seem like a bad idea.

"Come here...let's get you ready." Cooper's voice was soft and soothing. He probably had a really good guess what was going through my head. He liked to drive me nuts, but I never surprised him.

Taking a deep breath, I rolled over and went up onto all fours. Letting my body relax, I closed my eyes and waited. I was a quiet pup, and Cooper was used to it, so from the moment I felt the collar wrap around my neck, I knew I didn't have to say anything.

"I can't wait to get pretty collars from Jackson—if he becomes our master and all. I'm not completely delusional. I realize that it might not work out, but I refuse to go into it with that mindset. What happens if I hold back trying to be rational, and he thinks that means I don't like him? Nope, going all in, even though that makes you nervous." Cooper's hands started running long soothing strokes down my head and neck and onto my back.

It wasn't exactly a massage; it was more like you'd rub down a dog or horse. It was one of the little things that he knew helped me let everything go and just embrace my pup. It had been hard for me at first. Not because Cooper was seeing me so vulnerable, because I knew that was part of it, but pushing all the responsibilities away that seemed to pile up was so difficult.

There were always a thousand things that I should be doing. When we first started exploring the puppy-play lifestyle it had been thoughts about balancing out the meager savings I had and making sure we had enough food without going overboard. Letting everything stressful fade away had been one of the hardest things I'd ever done.

"I think you need a pretty collar with subtle designs, not flashy like mine will be." Much to Cooper's frustration, we'd gotten plain black leather collars for our puppy time. When we'd talked about it, the idea had been that Master, whoever he turned out to be, would pick out fancier ones for us.

The waiting was driving Cooper crazy.

Sometimes when he was bored, I'd find him searching for pictures online, trying to pick out the prettiest ones. When he'd discovered the fetish gear on the Leashes and Lace site, he'd obsessed over it for days.

To me, it was just like a name for my pup, something I was going to wait for.

Names were one of the other things that Cooper was convinced Master should give us too. I was on the fence about the whole thing when he first started explaining what he wanted, but I had to admit that the idea was starting to grow on me.

Cooper thought it was what should happen, but I thought that it would give our faceless Master a chance to feel like he was part of it too and not just a third on the outside watching our relationship.

By the time Cooper was ready for the next step, I was so relaxed and calm, I really didn't care what he was going to do. "Okay, turn around for me, pup."

There was usually a hint of longing in his voice, like Cooper would have loved to switch places with me, but it wasn't there this time. Maybe it was because he thought I needed it so much, but I had a feeling it was more about Jackson than anything else.

Master or not, Jackson had given him instructions and had taken control, giving Cooper something to follow and something to center him. No matter what the reason, I was going to be grateful and enjoy not having anything to worry about.

"Head down, pup." I'd have been embarrassed if it were anyone other than Cooper watching me, but I knew he loved me and how incredible it would be when everything was ready.

Letting my shoulders and head relax on the bed, I arched my back and sighed when his hand started flowing down my back and over my ass. The soothing touch continued as I heard the cap of the lube pop off. I'd never understood why people thought the sound of lube coming out was dirty or an embarrassing sound.

To me it was beautiful. The anticipation it built. Knowing what it meant, and the pleasure it was going to bring was wonderful. That sound meant I got to fly.

When Cooper's finger finally started circling my hole, I let my muscles relax and gave him a little whine. It wasn't much, but it was more than I usually did when we played, so Cooper knew how much I wanted it.

"That's a good pup. One day Master's going to play with us and see how beautiful you look. He'll love your pretty tail and how sweet you are." Cooper continued the tender words as he slid one finger in, slowly stretching me.

He took more time than he really needed, but considering I'd just come, the slow build was wonderful. By the time he'd added a second finger and brushed over my prostate, my cock was starting to twitch and think about joining the play.

I ignored it and soaked up the wonderful feelings running through me. The fullness of the plug as it slid in, the quiet, sweet words that streamed out of Cooper, the feel of his hand running up and down my legs and ass. It was peaceful and perfect. A warm buzz flowed through me, and I wanted to roll around in the feelings like they were a perfect scent that I had to keep close.

"All right, let's get you ready, and we'll go curl up on the couch, pup." Cooper went over to the closet and grabbed the special gloves that fit over my hands, making them feel like feet.

"The other day, Master asked if we had masks or the full outfits, and when I told him we didn't, he told me about some of the videos he watched. He said there were some incredible masks that were fascinating, but he liked being able to see the pup's reactions as they played and curled up with their master." Cooper continued to ramble through his thoughts as he fit the gloves onto my hands.

"He was okay with the idea of trying it if I was curious, but he laughed when I told him I liked being a naked kind of pup better. Master just joked if we ever played with other pups we might have to negotiate that." Cooper ran his hand over my back one last time before he reached for the leash I hadn't even noticed.

Hooking it on my collar, he stepped back. "All right, down, pup."

It was another layer that we didn't play with all the time, but I knew he got it out, so he would have a reason to talk to Jackson about it. As I climbed carefully off the bed, trying not to jostle my tail too much, he started talking through things again.

"I'm not sure how I feel about that. I know that a lot of other pups get together and play, but the idea was always so overwhelming before. Maybe with Jackson, it would be different. I'm going to have to think about that." Cooper kept talking like I was a real pup and wasn't expecting a response.

I was grateful for it because I had no idea how I would feel about it. And I wasn't going to worry over it anytime soon.

Sparks fired through me as the tip of the plug rubbed against my prostate. As I moved, the tail wagged, caressing just deep enough inside me to feel wonderful. It had been such a crazy sensation to get used to originally, but now it was fabulous. It was almost the same feeling as being fucked and sent a flood of submission through me, but knowing it was my tail made it even better.

It was all too jumbled up to explain, but it was perfect.

By the time we got to the couch, I couldn't have even told someone my name. I was simply Cooper's pup as I curled up beside him on the couch. Closing my eyes, I rested my head on his lap and made another soft whine as he started petting me slowly.

I drifted off to that place where nothing else mattered but the feel of his touch and the sound of his voice as he talked about how perfect his first date with Jackson had been. The last things I remembered for a long time were his fingers trailing over my head and his sweet words about how hot the kiss had been. Knowing it had been everything he'd dreamed of had tears prickling at my eyes, and I snuggled into him, perfectly content.

12

COOPER

I was awake entirely too early for even a workday, but I couldn't help it. Today was the day! "Sawyer?"

Getting him up was probably a bad idea, but I was too excited. "It's the day. Are you nervous? I might be, but I'm excited too, and I can't stop picturing how perfect it will be."

"Coop for the love of...go back to sleep. My date isn't for hours." Sawyer grumbled and rolled over, shoving his face into my neck.

"I can't help it. I'm so excited. You're going to have so much fun!" He was going on a date with Jackson! "You're gonna have dinner and it's going to be so much fun, and do you think he's going to take you out after you eat? What kind of burger place will it be? I've tried to look up different options, but I can't figure out which one because there's a few good possibilities, but I would have never guessed about the diner, so I'm not sure if it'll be someplace like that."

"Cooper, how much coffee have you had?" The words were low and not as frustrated as I would have guessed, so I smiled.

"None, I just got up. That sounds good, though. I'll make you one of the good ones. Lots of chocolate? Oh, and I got croissant dough at the store the other day. Do you want me to make you some? And eggs?" I was fighting dirty, but it was going to take something good to keep him from grumbling about getting up early.

"Maybe." He was slightly frustrated, but I could hear the interest in his voice. They were only the refrigerated croissants that I had to roll up, but he thought they were great. We'd had such basic things for so long that things like rolls and pastries were still fun. "Why are you so excited for my date? I was kind of worried you'd be jealous or something."

"Should I be?" I hadn't really looked at it like that. We'd talked about having a master and a third for so long, the idea seemed reasonable and not something to be jealous over. "Is my date on Saturday going to upset you?"

He snorted. "Hell, no. I'm going to sleep in and do absolutely nothing while he entertains you."

Laughing, I hugged him. "And I don't have to worry about you being bored while I'm at work or lonely. You're going to have someone to talk to and have fun with. It's perfect." The more I'd thought about his date, the more excited I'd become, and it was starting to feel like I was going to pop.

It was better than Christmas.

"Are you going to kiss him goodnight?" That wasn't really what I wanted to know, but I figured I'd start easy since he was still sleepy.

Sawyer didn't even think. "Hopefully."

"Do you want a knock-your-socks-off kiss too?"

It took him a little longer to answer—like he hadn't made up his mind. "Maybe."

He might have been nervous about how everything would work out, but I knew him well enough to know that he was more than ready for a kiss like that. "Do you think he's going to touch you and make you crazy? He spanked me last week."

Sawyer snorted again. "One swat doesn't count."

"It does too. Maybe if you tell him how good I've been, I'll get another. Or do you think we should tell him I've been naughty? Do you think that would work better? I'm not sure. Maybe we should let the too much caffeine and chocolate incident slip? It's not too bad, and he might even think it was funny."

Sawyer started laughing. Pulling away, he rolled to his side and propped his head up with one hand. "Do you want to go over his lap and have him pull your pants down? He could tell you how naughty you were and make your ass nice and pink?"

Nodding excitedly, I had to reach down and adjust my dick. "He'd have to. He thinks I'm too cute to say no to."

Sawyer started to chuckle again. "He said no to dessert last week."

"But that was different. He was watching out for me." *Duh.*

"I think he was watching out for me and him, but whatever." Smiling, he leaned over and gave me a kiss. "Good morning."

"It's Thursday." I still couldn't believe it was finally date day.

The week had seemed endless. No matter how many times I texted Jackson or how many phone calls we had, nothing made it go faster. Even teasing him and telling him in fabulous detail about how thoroughly I'd apologized to Sawyer hadn't made the week go by any quicker.

"Yes, it is." I knew he was looking forward to his date, but there was something in his eyes.

"What's wrong? Are you nervous?"

He sighed and curled into me again. "I'm just trying to imagine how it's going to work out."

"Work out what?"

"Like dating him and the puppy stuff and the physical side of things." Sawyer closed his eyes, and I wrapped my arms around him.

"He's not expecting to see us as pups until we're ready." He'd made that very clear. Sure, he was curious, that was perfectly normal, but rushing us into something wasn't his style.

Sawyer paused for a moment. "What if you're ready before me?"

I wasn't seeing the problem. Shrugging, I gave him a hug. "Then I'll be a pup and you won't."

"That wouldn't bother you? Or make him think I didn't trust him or something?"

"He really doesn't seem to mind that we need to go at different paces." I knew I was going to be ready to show him my pup before Sawyer was, and Jackson was probably expecting that. He read us both pretty well. Even on the phone, he knew we communicated differently. "And you're *you* a lot when I'm a pup, so it wouldn't be that different."

Jackson would flirt outrageously with me, but he took the time to work into things with Sawyer. Sawyer would blush and stumble through, eventually, but Jackson never rushed him. They were so much fun to watch, even though I could only see Sawyer's side of their conversation.

"Do you think he'd throw the ball for me?" I was a bouncy pup, and I wasn't sure how it would look to Jackson. Of course he was going to think I was cute, he'd already said he was curious about my tail, but the general excitement might be a bit much for him.

Sawyer looked up at me and smiled. "I think he's going love throwing the ball for you." Then he blushed a little and looked away. "Yesterday, he was telling me about a video he watched, and it was a guy playing with his pup. Jackson seemed... interested in it."

Interested meant turned-on, right?

Probably.

"He's going to love both our pups. One to play with and one

to cuddle. It's perfect." We were a fabulous match, and Jackson was going to see it right away. "Do you want to have sex with him tonight?"

That might have been too abrupt a change in topic for Sawyer, because his head went down, and he started coughing like I'd surprised him. It made sense to me. I wasn't sure why he hadn't expected that question, but evidently, it was a surprise to him.

Finally, Sawyer started to breathe normally, but he rolled over to look at the ceiling and not me. Interesting. He tried to sound normal when he spoke, but the tension and confusion in his voice was clear. "It's only our first date."

"Oh, no that math doesn't count. Between emails and phone calls and text messages that counts as at least one date, maybe two, and we had one together too, so conservative estimate is that this will be at least date three, if not four. See, perfectly acceptable sex date."

I liked how my math worked out.

We were not going to count my date on Saturday as my first date with Jackson. That was going to be like five because I was going to claim Sawyer's date with him too. Sex on the fifth date made us positively boring.

Sawyer laughed, and the tension started leaving his body. "Four dates is a long time not to see how the chemistry would be."

"Absolutely." And five dates would be torture. Also, I wasn't sure how to lead things from pancakes to sex. There didn't seem to be a good way to connect the two. But dinner, that was something else entirely. "Why don't you ask him over for coffee after dinner tonight? Nightcap? Dessert? I'm sure he'll get the idea."

Jackson wasn't stupid.

"You don't think it's too soon or that it will be weird?"

Sawyer's voice was filled with concern, but I didn't understand what he was upset about.

How would normal sex be weird? What did he want to do with Jackson?

Sawyer smiled and shook his head, realizing I wasn't following. "Like watching me doing stuff with him or him watching us? Would that upset you?"

"God no, that's going to be hot." I wiggled closer and slid my hard cock against his hip just in case he needed the proof. "I loved watching you two kiss the other day, and having you watch us was even more combustibler."

He snorted. "I'm not sure that's a word."

"It should be." Just picturing how it would go made my insides start to dance around. "It's going to be incredible."

"It's just that we've never done anything like this, and I don't want it to be weird for us." Sawyer was still worried, but it wasn't nearly as much as it'd been a few minutes ago.

"We were waiting for the right person." It was another "duh" sentence to me, but I restrained myself admirably. "We found him. It's not like we were going to jump into bed with someone weird or gross. He's funny and clearly likes us and had the patience to email us and make sure we knew what we were looking for."

Why would I want to wait?

"If it were just you and him on your third or fourth date, you can't tell me you wouldn't have thought about jumping into bed with him." I gave Sawyer a disbelieving look. He'd been a horny thing in high school, so there was no way I was buying any line of shit.

He laughed and shook his head. "Of course not, but this is—"

I broke in. "It's just the same. We're seeing how he fits in our relationship and in our family. Same thing."

Sitting up, Sawyer leaned close and gave me a kiss. "Then yes. I thought about having sex with him and inviting him back here."

A shiver raced through me. "I could walk in, and you'd be naked on the couch while he played with you waiting for me to come home. You'd be desperate and needy and so ready to be fucked it'd be amazing."

I had a *fabulous* imagination.

Sawyer's eyes got wider, and he licked his lips, nodding slowly, clearly agreeing. "Maybe."

"Do you remember that porn movie where the Dom had one of his boys on his lap with a cock ring on the sub to keep his cock hard and the boy was stuffed with his Dom's dick and had to keep his master hard while they waited for the other guy to come home?" I thrust my hips and ran my own erection against Sawyer's hip again.

We'd "researched" threesomes and ménage relationships until all that was left was porn and then we'd "studied" that too. That movie was one we'd seen a thousand times because the scene was so hot it just about melted the computer.

Sawyer leaned down and gave me a heated, scorching kiss. "You're trying to kill me."

"But it would be a fabulous way to go." He'd look so hot like that. Desperate and needy, waiting to come until he got permission.

"How about we stick with coffee and kisses until you come home and then we'll see?"

"So boring. But I'll take it." Then I frowned as a thought occurred to me. "What if he doesn't want to have sex yet?"

Sawyer laughed and shrugged. "I don't see how that's possible, but if he's not ready, then we won't rush him."

"No rushing. But if he wants to wait for sex, you'll fuck me tonight and pretend he's watching us?" Just the idea that we might make love with Jackson tonight was going to make me crazy all day, and someone was going to need to fuck me later, or I'd explode.

Sawyer grinned wickedly and rolled on top of me, pinning me to the bed. "Of course."

He had me beautifully trapped against the mattress, but I stretched my neck up and kissed him. When Sawyer pulled back, shaking his head, I started to pout. "Not this morning. I think Master would want you all hard and needy today."

He was so mean and so perfect. "You think?"

Sawyer nodded. "He'd love it."

No matter how Jackson would really feel, the fantasy was hot. "You're just trying to get back at me for driving you crazy."

He grinned. "Possibly. But it's still sexy."

I couldn't argue with that. "But no matter what, I get pounded-into-the-mattress sex later?"

"We can even pretend he's fucking you up against a wall. Remember how he held you up? He's strong enough that he could do it." Sawyer's voice dropped, so it was husky and erotic. "He'd pound into you, and you'd feel it for days."

The fantasy was so erotic and tempting, it was all I could do not to thrust up into him and grind against him until I exploded. It wouldn't take long. In seconds, I could be exploding as my orgasm shot through me. But Sawyer shook his head like he knew what I was thinking and climbed off me. "Wasn't I promised coffee since you woke me up early?"

Every bit of blood in my body was in my cock, and my brain was fried. And he wanted coffee? I wasn't going to get a damned thing done today.

As he jumped off the bed, dick hard and sticking out in front of him like a beacon, he started heading toward the bathroom. "Coffee, Coop. You promised."

I sank back onto the bed. Sawyer was going to have to wait

until I could walk. As I lay there listening to him in the bathroom, I started thinking about their date. Sawyer liked to tease that my thinking was dangerous. He was probably right, but that didn't mean it wasn't a good idea.

Why wait all day to figure out if Jackson wanted sex when I could just text him?

13

JACKSON

After waking up to Cooper's text message, the rest of the day had been a total loss. Even the dogs had sensed my excitement and had been particularly wound up. I couldn't decide if Sawyer knew what the little scamp had done or not.

I was betting he didn't. He would have been much more nervous otherwise. Not that he was calm by any means. But by the time we'd finished our burgers and were poring over the dessert menu, he was smiling and leaning back in the booth, nowhere near as nervous as he'd been when I picked him up.

"Are you going to happen to mention that you got dessert tonight?" I couldn't resist laughing at Sawyer's emphatic nod.

"Of course." Sawyer smirked. "He deserves it."

Now that was curious. Cooper had assured me he'd been absolutely perfect this week. He kept taunting me with all kinds of questions about rewards and how good he really needed to be. "What did he do? He was telling me how well-behaved he was this week." I had to smile. "His words, not mine."

And Sawyer went purple again.

It didn't happen frequently, but every so often, I'd hit on a topic or say something that made him blush brilliantly, and he'd stumble around for a moment. Most of the time, he'd manage to tell me what got such a good reaction, even when I wasn't expecting an answer.

Honesty seemed to be a big deal in his relationship with Cooper, and I wasn't sure what it meant that I was afforded it too. Was it with everyone? Or just someone he was in a relationship with?

Sawyer breathed in deeply, and then reached for his glass and took a long drink of water. When there weren't any more good reasons to put it off, he finally started to speak. "Cooper was trying to drive me crazy and might have said some things about telling you that he'd been good and rewards and stuff."

Ahh.

"I got something along those lines in some texts. Along with several questions about what kinds of things could get him punished. Could. Not would. I, um, got the message with those." And if we were being honest, I needed to make sure he was aware of Cooper's texts from earlier. "Along with a very interesting question first thing this morning."

Sawyer's eyes widened and swallowed nervously. "How early?"

"Before six. I didn't see it until I got up later, but...he was asking a question I'm starting to think you weren't aware of. It was very matter-of-fact. And polite. He said that he hoped he didn't wake me up, but he wanted to know my opinion on sleeping with someone on the third or fourth date. Then something I didn't understand about texts counting as a date."

"Lord, Coop." Sawyer closed his eyes. "He, um, thought that the emails and stuff should count as a date, so he's counting this as our third date."

I gestured between Sawyer and myself. "Our third date or all of us?" I wasn't sure I was following the math.

Sawyer laughed, starting to relax. He pushed his dessert menu away and rested one elbow on the table, smiling. "He said he got to claim this one as well. So, third or fourth, depending on how the texts and stuff counted. He was petitioning to count them as two."

"So that's why he was so excited when I messaged back." The flood of emojis and confusing text speech that didn't contain nearly enough vowels let me know he was excited, but not why he was so thrilled.

"Um, what did you say to him?" Sawyer's face grew blank, and he glanced down at the table. He looked like he wasn't sure if he wanted to know the answer or not.

I didn't want to lie, but I also wasn't sure if telling him the truth would make him uncomfortable or not. "I told him that I thought the third date was perfectly reasonable for knowing if you wanted to sleep with someone as long as the people, the couple…group…as long as everyone was on the same page."

Sawyer nodded slowly, and I saw his teeth start pulling at his bottom lip. Unsure how he was feeling, I kept going. "Are we all on the same page?"

Slowly, his head came up, and he looked at me, shrugging. "I don't know."

He was nervous, but I had to smile. "Cooper certainly knows."

Sawyer laughed, his wide smile shining. "Cooper is very sure of what he wants." Then Sawyer gave me a serious look. "You."

Shaking my head, I corrected him. "Us. He wants us. You two are a family. That's what he keeps telling me, and I can see that whenever you even talk about each other."

"But there are things that he wants—that *we* want, and we need someone with us." Sawyer's nervous honesty was endearing but didn't make the conversation any clearer.

"What happens when he's more ready than you are?" Was that what he was worried about?

Sawyer was honest to a fault. "I *might* be ready. It's just a big step."

"You guys have never..." I flicked my hand back and forth, not sure how to ask if they'd ever invited someone else into their bedroom.

"No. We were waiting for the right guy."

"Have you found the right guy?" I threw the question out there and then waited to see what he said.

"You boys decide what you want for dessert? Jackson, you always get the apple pie and vanilla ice cream, so I don't even know why you're still looking."

We both jumped like a spider had landed right on the table. Alice looked at us like we were insane. "You boys all right?"

"Yes, sorry. I think we've worked out dessert. Sawyer, do you need another minute?"

He shook his head, looking down at the menu and then back up at Alice. She was an older woman who'd looked the same since I first started coming in years before. She never changed. Slightly impatient with a sharp tongue and long white hair that was always in a bun on the back of her head, she fit the atmosphere of the place.

Sawyer had been skeptical when we'd first walked in. The restaurant was in a bit of a transitional part of town, but considering it had been there for years, most of the regulars didn't notice. When he'd seen the size of the burgers and how perfect the fries were, he made his apologies.

"No, I'm good. I'm going to get the lemon meringue." Alice reached for his menu, and he smiled. "Thank you."

"The usual, Jackson?" She gave me a look like even asking that question was ridiculous.

"No, I think I'd like to try the S'mores pie you said was so good."

Her eyes opened, and she looked between Sawyer and me. "Trying new things, I see." Then she nodded and walked away.

"Was that…" Sawyer didn't seem to know what to say. "Does she know you're gay?"

"Yes." I'd never hidden it, and I knew how fortunate I was when it came to that part of my life. "She tried to fix me up with her daughter when I first started coming in. When I explained about being gay, she dragged a nephew over who she said was on the fence and needed someone to talk to."

"Did you date him?" Sawyer was smiling and curious. A bit of his age showing and maybe his outlook on things in general, because there was no judgment or awkwardness from potentially asking about someone who might have been an old boyfriend.

I shook my head. "He was young, but a very innocent young if you know what I mean. The dynamics were wrong. I did have several long talks with him and gave him his first kiss from a man. He's married to a dentist now, and they have two kids. Alice normally gives me updates and even pulls out the pictures, but I guess she could tell that it wouldn't be that appropriate to do in front of you."

"We look like we're…dating, huh?" I wasn't exactly sure what to call us either, but his label worked for now. Especially in public.

"I think so. Does that bother you?"

He shook his head decisively. "No, neither Cooper or I want to keep our…the person we're dating hidden away once it's serious. I work behind the scenes, and I'm hoping my boss won't notice until I'm a little higher up in the company. And Cooper's boss is really open-minded, so I don't think we have anything to worry about. What about you? Eventually, we're going to run into one of your clients."

I wasn't going to deny the thought had fazed me just a little, but I thought it was worth the risk. "I'm ready to settle down, and I'm past the point where the preconceived notions about how I thought a relationship should look matters. I might end up shocking some of my clients, but for the most part, I don't remember the last time one of them asked me about who I was dating, or if I was even married. We keep the classes and training sessions focused on the dogs. I don't think that will change. And for the people who matter in my life, they're going to be a little surprised, but that's about it. Not that I plan on disclosing everything. I think some parts of our relationship should remain private unless we are in very specific situations."

I know it was something we'd already discussed, but I wanted us both clear on that. The BDSM aspect and the puppy-play lifestyle were things that I didn't need to share with anyone. Especially people who wouldn't get it.

"Cooper said you guys talked about going to meetings or events that are into...well, you know." He glanced around the restaurant, trying to make sure we weren't being too loud.

"We did. I'm on the fence. I think I'm going to have to see how it feels between the three of us first. I'm not pushing the idea completely aside, though. From what I've read, it's a very social scene." And not necessarily overwhelmingly sexual. There seemed to be a variety of ways people embraced the scene, and some made me more comfortable than others.

Sawyer nodded. "I think it would be more of Cooper's thing than mine, but maybe..." His voice trailed off and he shrugged. I was kind of at the same place mentally, so I nodded.

"It's not something we have to figure out anytime soon." Before I could add anything else, Alice was back with our desserts.

She was still shaking her head. "Must be the end of times if you're not getting apple pie." Then she glanced at Sawyer and gave him a long look. "You must be good for him, sweetie."

Sawyer blushed and looked away, mumbling a low thank-you that made her smile as she walked away. I laughed. "She likes you."

He picked up his fork and turned his gaze to me. "Will she like me when she eventually meets Cooper?"

"I think so. She's never going to let me eat apple pie again, though."

He grinned. "Not so vanilla anymore."

"It looks that way." I wasn't sure if he was going to turn the conversation back to where it had been headed before Alice interrupted or if I needed to be the one to bring it up. BDSM rules seemed to vary between couples, and I wasn't sure where they stood on the more take-charge aspect of the lifestyle outside of the bedroom.

Neither one of them had an issue when I made the dessert decision last time, but everything else was still up in the air. Once Sawyer was a little more comfortable, we needed more discussions. And making a list might not be a bad idea.

I must have looked odd, because he grinned at me and cocked his head. "What were you thinking?"

Smiling, I shrugged. "About making a list of questions and topics I want to discuss with you guys at some point. BDSM things, for the most part."

Clearly not expecting that answer, his fork tilted, and the bite of pie slipped off the end back onto the plate. "Oh, um, that's good. There are probably lots of questions going through your mind."

"Yes, most can wait until we're all more comfortable. But I need you to be honest and tell me if I'm overstepping my bounds, or if I'm giving you more room than you want. It's going to take me a while to understand how much of a master you're really looking for." Every time I said the word or talked about the lifestyle, it got easier, but I still worried that I sounded like a vanilla geek trying to talk to the cool kids.

Sawyer didn't seem to think it came across as ridiculous, because he nodded and shifted in his seat a little. Poking at his pie, he focused on the table. "Asking for more is going to be hard for me, but I'm betting Cooper runs his mouth enough that you'll know what I need. But I am going to try. Consent and everything, but it's not that easy."

"I can understand that." Taking a bite, I tried to give him some space to relax again and sort out his thoughts.

After a few more minutes and the last half of his pie, he glanced up at me again. "You know, Cooper would probably love a piece of that chocolate layer cake on the menu."

"All that ganache and icing will have him bouncing off the walls."

"Yes, but if you stopped by the house for a while tonight and gave it to him, I'm sure his thank-you would be memorable." Sawyer blushed a little. "He certainly took your instructions about apologizing to me very seriously."

"I heard, in long, torturously detailed texts. He even managed to bring it up in two different phone calls." If the coffee shop job ever fell through, I was going to encourage him to go into writing. He'd make a fortune selling erotica.

Sawyer gave a low laugh. "He said he was going to."

"And you didn't object?" Cooper had implied that Sawyer knew, and I was guessing that it was something that they'd discussed, but I'd wanted to be sure.

Sawyer glanced down at his empty plate and pushed his fork through the crumbs. "No. He, um, made it sound like sharing it with you was a good idea."

Considering that we both knew Cooper's focus had been Sawyer, he had to have known that Cooper would describe every sexy detail about Sawyer's reactions. I wasn't ashamed to say that I'd jerked off for days to the images he'd put in my head.

"I think bringing him back dessert will be a good idea." Then I reached over and took Sawyer's free hand, wrapping mine around his. "But just because he's excited and ready, doesn't mean you have to be. Is that all right with you?"

How was I supposed to ask if it was okay if I had sex with Cooper?

Cooper's texts had been getting more and more X-rated, and while I loved it, I knew he wasn't going to be satisfied with just a kiss on the cheek. Sawyer flashed me a wicked grin. "He is certainly excited. And ready."

And that still hadn't answered my question.

Was it a Dom moment, or was I supposed to let Sawyer talk it out in his own time? They really needed to make a Cliffs Notes version of what they wanted in a master and a boyfriend. "How will you feel if Cooper takes things further than you're comfortable with? I'm assuming you want to be there and...watch?"

The conversation was starting to delve into new territories for me.

Sawyer took pity on me though and didn't make me figure out another way to ask. He nodded slowly and watched me carefully. "For right now, we do things like that together. Eventually, it will be different, but to begin with, I want to be there. And I'm good with Cooper being the focus. If I want to join in for more than kissing and stuff, I'll let you know."

"I don't want to guess wrong and upset anyone or push you into something you're not ready for. If you need to take a step back with whatever is happening, I want you to do it, and don't worry. I'll be more hurt if you don't let me know there's a problem."

"So, safeword time?" He looked skeptical. "I know we're not planning on doing anything crazy, but just to be sure?"

"Yes." That would be a great idea. "Stoplight system for now since that's what I've read about the most, but eventually, we can work out our own."

"Deal." Sawyer looked nervous still, but more relieved. "Are you ready to head back to our place, or was there something else you wanted to do tonight?"

"I'm not sure what movies are playing or anything, but why don't we head back to your place now and figure out something to do this weekend? After he gets off work later that night, maybe?" There were endless things to do around the city. We just needed to look for some options that would appeal to everyone.

"Sounds good. There are a few new movies out, but Cooper would pout if we saw one of his favorites without him." Sawyer laughed. "I don't want to live with that for the next week."

"I'll have to make sure I have a good bribe ready if we end up doing something like that without him then."

"Or a good punishment." Sawyer blushed a little but pushed through. "He'd, um, probably like that too."

I had to nod and grin. "I got a few emails that spelled that out *very* clearly."

"He's just a *little* excited."

"And not worried about jumping in right away." Cooper had so many fantasies and desires that he'd shared; I wasn't sure where to start first. Nothing was crazy or too much, but I wanted to make it perfect for him.

Sawyer shrugged. "I say let him jump in. He didn't have much of a dating life before we became a family, so I think you should give him everything you think he'd want."

"Why didn't he date much?" There were so many questions I wanted to ask, but I wasn't sure what would be a land mine and what would be an innocent topic. Just the little things they'd said made it clear they didn't have anyone else.

"His parents were really conservative. They didn't come right out and say anything about him being gay, but they made it clear he was too young to date and things like that. I think they probably would have been just as nuts if he'd been straight, but they seemed to be even more careful with him after he came out." Sawyer took a sip of his water and started playing with his fork again.

"He didn't push back because he realized he was different from the other gay guys he knew. I explained stuff as best I could, but I was still figuring some things out, so it never occurred to me to talk to him about kinkier stuff." Another drink gave Sawyer a few seconds to gather his thoughts. "By the time he was ready to date and explore things, his parents put a hold on anything they saw as dating. I was only allowed near him because he said we were just friends, and we never gave them any reason not to believe it. We were just buddies then."

"I bet you were there for him more than any other friend would have been." Just from hearing him talk and the look on his face, that was obvious.

Sawyer smiled. "He was so innocent when he started high school and so small I had to stick close to keep him out of trouble."

I was starting to get the idea that we were heading into trickier territory with the story, so I was glad when Alice came up to the table again. "You boys ready for the check?"

"Yes, ma'am, but can I get a piece of the chocolate cake to go?"

She gave me a long look. "You that hungry?"

Laughing, I shook my head and decided to go for it. She wasn't going to let it drop, anyway. "No, Cooper's waiting for us at their house"—I gestured to a wide-eyed Sawyer—"because he had to work late, so this will be a nice surprise."

The wily old woman gave me a knowing look. "Nice to think of his roommate."

"No, he's our other boyfriend." And it was out.

Sawyer was waiting for the ceiling to come crashing down, but she grinned. "I got a book like that at home. I'll get you boys a big piece to take to your fella."

Alice walked off, still grinning and mumbling something about how she wished things had been different back in her day. I had to laugh. She'd have been hell on wheels when she was young no matter what the social norms had been then.

Shaking his head and clearly trying to figure out what had happened, Sawyer watched her walk away. He and Cooper must have had a difficult time growing up, but I was glad he was getting to see that there were people out there who wouldn't care.

And then there were dirty old ladies who were going to have entirely too much fun caring.

"I think I'm going to have to get some book recommendations from Melissa. Maybe even Alice too."

Sawyer laughed and shook his head. "Don't forget to ask Cooper. He's got dirty stuff on that phone of his—ebooks, pictures, everything you could think of. We don't ever let him open picture apps in public...if you get my drift."

"That doesn't surprise me at all." I looked over at Alice who was starting to head back in our direction. Giving his hand one last squeeze, I reached over and ran a finger down his cheek, trying to convey without words everything that was going through my head. "You ready to go home?"

His smile that time was tender and seemed more confident, but I hoped I wasn't just seeing what I wanted to. His thumb ran over the back of my hand, that little touch sending shivers up my spine, and he nodded. "Yes, I'm ready."

14

SAWYER

I'd given up trying to figure out if I was making the right decision. I was just going to shove my brain out the window and let my instincts take over. Heart, stomach, dick...they were all in favor of throwing myself at Jackson and giving my best impression of a horny Cooper.

The drive home didn't make it any easier either.

Cradling Cooper's cake gave my hands something to do, but it left my brain free to wander. And obsess. When I started our date, I was convinced I wasn't ready for anything beyond making out. Certainly nothing like what Cooper was fantasizing over. But as the date had gone on, I'd started becoming less and less sure.

I knew it was more about the fear of what might happen than not being ready for sex, but sorting it all out in my head was impossible. It was easy to tell Cooper what I wanted a master to do to him and to me when it was a vague distant figure that we just teased each other with.

Now Master had a face.

That seemed to make everything more real and harder to deal with. I didn't want to hide from what I needed or desired.

I'd moved past that in high school when I realized that "bottom" and "submissive" weren't the same thing.

Jackson reached out to turn the radio down and then let his hand rest on my leg. "You seem nervous."

Right to the issue. "I am."

No point in trying to lie about that. In our family, we didn't hide things from each other. And if there was even the possibility of him becoming a permanent part of our family, then that meant honesty with him too. "I'm not a hundred percent sure what I want, so that's making it hard."

"I can understand that. I don't think it's something we have to decide right now, though." His fingers absently caressed my leg as he weaved through the traffic, and I knew he wasn't aware of what he was doing.

"One step at a time?"

He chuckled. "I was thinking more about Cooper. I can't see him sticking to any plans we make."

Laughing, I nodded and scooted my leg closer to encourage his touch. His hand tightened, and I relaxed back in the seat. "I have a good guess about what he'll do since you said you were good to go on the third date."

He grinned. "Hey, in my defense, I was counting dates separately, so his third date wouldn't have happened until later."

Jackson didn't seem like he minded in the least, so I didn't make excuses for Cooper. Jackson seemed to honestly like him the way he was—bouncy, open, and loving. Jackson was everything I would have picked out for Cooper. If I'd been shopping for the perfect Dom, I couldn't have found a better match. I just couldn't believe that he was perfect for me too.

It was a little frightening.

Waiting for the other shoe to drop was exhausting.

The weight of his hand as it ran up and down my leg was almost hypnotic. By the time we finally pulled into the parking lot, I was sinking into the seat and my cock had decided that it liked the almost innocent touch on my thigh.

My dick liked everything about him.

Parking, Jackson looked over at me as he opened the door. "Let me come around and open that for you. So you don't drop the cake."

Smiling at his poorly disguised manners, I nodded. If he wanted to open it, I wasn't going to argue. Watching him walk around the car, I let my eyes wander over his body. Even in jeans and a sweater, he looked incredible. The way the material stretched over his broad, muscular body made my mouth water.

Cooper called him yummy. Cooper was right.

As he opened the door, he held out one hand to help me up. Ever the gentleman. If I hadn't seen some of his texts with Cooper, I would've never believed the man in front of me was behind the sexy texts that teased Cooper with the wicked fantasies that were running through his head.

"Thank you."

"You're welcome." He was so close I had to move the cake to the side, or it would have been squished between us. "Would it bother you if I kissed you now?"

"Some of our neighbors are going to be surprised, but I don't mind." I leaned closer and felt his body brush against mine. "But wouldn't you rather wait until we got upstairs?"

He was still coming, right?

I got a tender smile, and one hand came up to cup my face. "I want to give you a goodnight kiss here first. So you know that no matter what happens later, I had a wonderful time and nothing is going to change that."

So stinkin' cute.

Nodding because I wasn't sure my voice would work, I brought my free hand up and wrapped it around his neck. I stretched a little and met his mouth as it came down to touch mine. His lips were warm and full, and I loved the strength that seemed to flow from him. His touch was sure, and he let the kiss start out gentle and almost chaste.

Before it had a chance to deepen, he pulled away. "I had a wonderful time with you tonight. Thank you for coming to dinner with me, Sawyer."

"Thank you for asking me." It seemed silly and almost juvenile, but I wanted him to know that I appreciated the effort that he'd made. "Thank you for doing something special with me."

That tender smile widened, and he leaned down and kissed my forehead. "I like the idea of doing things with both of you and each of you separately. I want you to know that you're important to me together and as individuals."

Not knowing how to respond and not sound sappy, I smiled and leaned in to give him another kiss. "No more making out in the parking lot. We live in an accepting neighborhood, but I'll never live it down if our neighbors find us doing interesting things."

"*Interesting*, huh?"

Grinning, I shrugged. "Once Cooper gets involved."

Jackson laughed and took my hand. Stepping back, he let me move away from the car, and I shut the door. He locked it, and we started heading for the stairs, still holding hands. When he'd picked me up earlier, he didn't see much of the apartment, so I was curious about what he was going to think.

As we started walking up the stairs, he turned to me. "When is Cooper getting home?"

"Not sure. He was texting non-stop until he started going over stuff with his manager and then it went quiet. I'm not sure if he's going to go crazy texting once he leaves or not." Cooper was great about not doing anything stupid when he was driving, but stoplights might be fair game when he was excited. "I didn't see the car in the parking lot, though."

Sharing a car was hard, but neither of us wanted two car

payments yet. We'd talked about it before he started looking at going to school, but once he made up his mind, that pushed car buying back again. We wanted as little debt as possible until he had the promotion, and we saw how expensive college was really going to be.

Reaching the apartment, I dug out my keys and opened the door. As we walked in, I shut the door and started pointing out things. "Bedroom is down that way and kitchen is over there. It's small but—"

"Hey, it's better than my first three apartments. No buts."

"Your first *three*?"

"It took me a while to figure out what I wanted to do, so I was perpetually broke for about five years." He shrugged. "My first couple of places were sketchy, and I wouldn't even let my mother see the second one. She would have dragged my ass back home so fast my head would have spun."

"Protective?" Setting the cake down on the coffee table we'd gotten at a local thrift store, I looked at the place with new eyes. It was pretty nice. We'd done a great job picking out things that went together and haunting online ads and secondhand shops.

"You have no idea." He laughed and sat down on the couch, casually pulling me down on his lap and wrapping his arms around me. "She makes a momma bear look calm and rational."

"Is she going to be okay with us?" I made a vague gesture with my hand trying to indicate Cooper too. "And how did you keep her away?"

He laughed and tightened his hold. "She said as long as Melissa approved, it would be just fine, and she wouldn't pester me. Well, what she didn't know was that Mellie was dating some guy with a motorcycle and big hair that looked like something from an '80s biker movie. Shady as hell, but he seemed to be nice to her, so I didn't rat her out. But the deal was that she'd keep my secret if I kept hers."

"I take it she keeps secrets pretty good?" Curling into him, I let one hand start tracing circles on his chest. It had been so long since anyone but Cooper had held me, it was almost strange. But in a good way—like the rush right before a roller coaster starts the climb up to the top.

Fear.

Excitement.

An almost passionate heat that flooded through the rider, then right before you reached the top, in that split second before you went over it was incredible. I was on my roller coaster, and the moment was beautiful.

Jackson snorted and relaxed back into the couch, pulling me with him so we were pressed even tighter together. "Better than I thought. I honestly had no idea about the writing thing. Maybe it's selfish, but I don't know why she didn't trust me. I wouldn't have told, and I would have supported her."

Lifting my head, I gave his cheek a kiss. "It's probably just really personal for her. I knew this guy in high school who wrote stories and stuff. He never let me read that many, but even the fiction ones that looked nothing like his real life were almost like his kids. He said there was a piece of him inside the story. Maybe she's the same way?"

He'd been a passionate little thing. A smaller guy physically, everyone had assumed he was gay for years, but he never said anything in high school about his preferences. I only knew because I caught him watching me taking a piss one time, and he knew he'd been caught.

I was young enough that I thought small twink meant bottom, never mind the fact that I didn't conform to the stereotype, so I wasn't particularly interested. But boy was I wrong. He must have understood better than I had that looks didn't always have to match what was inside, because the next week he'd cornered me behind the school and had fucked me nearly senseless.

Until Cooper changed from friend to family, my little top

had been one of the only guys I'd actually thought about getting serious with. He'd moved away senior year, but he'd been someone who really made me understand I wasn't just a bottom, but that there was something more I was searching for.

"I hadn't really thought of it that way." Jackson's hands started caressing my leg again in long, slow strokes. I wanted to squirm and press myself closer. "Maybe."

"Have you talked to her about what she writes, besides the puppy play I mean?" Cooper had all kinds of books on that app, so I wasn't sure if he'd read anything she'd written. Saying he had eclectic tastes would have been an understatement.

"No, we've talked a couple of times, but she always ends up distracting me by asking about you guys. Then before I know it, she's off the phone, and I still don't know what she writes or even how it's going. She could be a bestselling author and I wouldn't know it." Just listening to him talk, it was clear that was more important than what she wrote or how kinky it was. He was hurt that he couldn't celebrate her successes with her.

"I'm sure she's just working up the nerve to tell you."

He sighed, and it was almost a pout. "She's got brass balls. She's probably just trying to torture me."

They seemed to have an interesting relationship, so that was probably possible. "But she doesn't mind you dating us? It's still weird that she knows about everything."

Jackson shook his head and gave me a quick peck. "She can't wait to meet you. I think everyone is going to love you both. It will be a bit of a surprise, but I'm not picturing anything crazy. Now my mother is going to kill me for not telling her sooner, but I wanted to make sure we were all on the same page first and that it was…you know…serious for you guys before I got her hopes up. She's been pushing me to settle down for ages."

"You're going to tell her about us?" Cooper and I didn't have the best track record when it came to families, so the idea made me a little nauseous. If I'd thought it through, I would have realized a family as close as Jackson's would eventually figure it out, but still...

"Of course." It seemed to take him a minute to mentally connect the dots. We hadn't told him much about our families, but he seemed like he could fill in the blanks pretty well, because he gave me a tender smile and brought me close for another kiss.

When he pulled back, he cupped my face again. "We have nothing to worry about from them. Aside from some slightly awkward questions, eventually they're going to love you. All I have to do is tell my mother I'm settling down with two wonderful men, and she's going to be over the moon."

Leaning in, he started sprinkling kisses around my face as he spoke. "You're smart and resourceful, and you love Cooper unconditionally, and you're honest and you're sexy, and you're open to love even though things were hard. They're going to love you."

There was something unspoken in his eyes, and it made my insides start to whirl again.

Shifting, I turned my body, so I was facing his and gave him a kiss. It wasn't just a thank-you for the sweet words or a kiss good night after a perfect date. It was permission.

And thank God he understood.

He took control of the kiss, and in a heartbeat, he'd turned it to something passionate and deep. His tongue flicked against my lips, and I opened, letting him take everything he wanted. It was one of those "Why was I fighting this?" moments. Like the first time I accepted I was submissive, or the first time Cooper talked me into trying out his puppy-play fantasy.

It was the rush of the roller coaster as I went zooming down the other side at a breakneck speed. His hands seemed to be everywhere at once as his mouth took mine. My back. My hip.

When it wasn't enough, I started to make low begging noises and grinding my ass into his thick cock.

He pulled back from the kiss, and his hands moved to my hips. As he started to move me around, I knew what he wanted. Straddling his legs, I sat back down and started grinding my dick against his. He gave a low, deep chuckle, and his hands moved down to cup the bottom of my ass.

I moaned into his mouth as he kissed me again, writhing on his lap and trying to plead for more. His lips were strong and soft, but his fingers were teasing and wicked. They kneaded my cheeks and slowly inched toward my hole. My clothes barely registered; all I wanted was to feel his touch, but he made me wait.

Little whines and pleading noises just made him smile wickedly and shake his head. "Not yet."

They were beautiful, perfect words. He was taking control. There were no decisions to make. Nothing to worry over. Jackson was going to handle everything. All I had to do was follow his lead. With safewords in place and a loving master's arms around me, there was nothing I had to do.

When I was shaking and so hard I knew there was no way he could miss it, his fingers crossed that last distance, and I felt the lightest touch move over the sensitive skin. But there were too many layers between us, and I knew from the look on his face, the passion and the fire, that he was nowhere near ready for me to come.

"So beautiful. God. So sexy." His mouth moved down to start kissing along my jaw and neck. The feel of his teeth as he nibbled on the long column and the texture of his tongue as he soothed the bite marks had me frantically thrusting back and forth between the pleasure.

Cock.

Ass.

Teeth.

I couldn't decide what I wanted more, and the knowledge that it wasn't up to me was incredible. I was Jackson's, and he would decide. The sexiest sentence ever.

But even knowing it wasn't my decision didn't stop me from begging and crying out for more.

"You brought me cake!" The excited sound of Cooper's voice had us springing apart like two kids caught necking on the couch.

I would have fallen on my ass if it wasn't for Jackson's great reflexes and strong grip. He gave a low laugh and fell back against the couch. I turned to Cooper, resting my head on Jackson's shoulder while my heartbeat went slowly back to normal. "Is that all you noticed?"

He plopped down next to us on the couch and smiled but reached out to pick up the clear plastic container, looking at it longingly before setting it down on the table. "Oh, you two are hot, but you brought me dessert from your date. It's so sweet."

He was so calm about Jackson and me; it was almost anticlimactic. But then out came the Cooper I knew and loved. "I'm just going to have to show both of you how grateful I am." Then with a wicked smile, he turned and sat up on his knees, giving us both kisses as he almost climbed on top of us.

The feel of his body against mine and the strength of Jackson's arms as they wrapped around us had the rush of need flooding back. When Cooper finally took a breath, he looked at both of us with passion and desire clearly on display, holding nothing back. "Do I need to get a shower now, or am I just going to get dirtier later?"

15

COOPER

It took a moment for my question to sink through. Either they were very out of it and still turned-on, or it hadn't made sense. I thought it was pretty straightforward, though. Finally Jackson smiled and pulled me in for another kiss.

Sawyer shook his head. "Coop, I love you."

That was sweet but didn't answer the question. Before I could point that out, Jackson broke in. "You will definitely need a shower later."

Yes!

"I will?" I wanted to be very clear about that. I was getting sex, right?

Jackson must have seen the question on my face, because he nodded and leaned in to give me another kiss. But the way his hand came up to cup the back of my head and the strength and passion behind the kiss, it felt more like he was taking it rather than giving.

Relief flooded through me. When he'd said he thought third-date sex was reasonable as long as everyone was fine with it, I'd worried all day that Sawyer wasn't going to be okay with it. I knew he wanted it. Everything in him seemed to respond when

I talked about Jackson as we were making love. But something was holding him back.

I wasn't sure if it was fear that Jackson was going to change his mind—or something about letting everything go and giving up control to him. But looking at him in Jackson's arms, I didn't see the turmoil inside him anymore.

When he finally released my lips, his hand kept a tight hold on my hair and he turned my head so I was facing Sawyer. "I think Sawyer needs a kiss too, doesn't he? I haven't seen how sexy my boys look together."

Fuck. That was hot.

Jumping right in, I said the first thing that came to mind. "Yes, Master."

They both moaned as my lips touched Sawyer's, and I felt Jackson's hand tighten on my head. The rush of sensation had me even harder than I'd gotten when I'd first walked in the door and had seen them making out.

I'd pictured them all day as being naked and beautifully on display when I got home—so seeing everyone's clothes on was kind of frustrating. But I'd known right away they'd been waiting on me to move things along.

They were so damned lucky to have me.

"You two..." Jackson couldn't seem to finish the rest of the sentence, but I could hear the desire in his voice as he watched us.

Moaning into Sawyer's mouth, I rocked my hips forward and arched out. I needed more. Jackson's hand moved down my back slowly, and it sent shivers through me. I pictured everything he could do as I poured all the need I was feeling into Sawyer's kiss.

As his fingers got closer and closer to my ass, his commands got more heated. "Arch that pretty ass out, Cooper. Let me see how much you want it."

Jackson must have done something to Sawyer, because he

gasped into my mouth and started kissing me even deeper, needier. Jackson's voice was hot and rough. "More, Sawyer. Show me how much you need him…how much you want to taste him. You want to please me, don't you?"

Sawyer took my mouth like he was at his most commanding, the sweetly erotic words pushing him higher, but I knew it was all for Jackson, so it got tangled up—the domination and submission in my head making everything sexier.

When Jackson's hand came down hard on my ass, the sensation sent desire flooding through me. Pushing back for more of the beautiful pleasure, I pulled back and cried out for him. "Master!"

"Keep kissing. I'm not done watching my sexy boys. But I think you're going to need to be punished, Cooper. You've been naughty this week. Teasing Sawyer and me, telling us all the wicked things you wanted to do with us. And now you're even disobeying me. What are you supposed to be doing, Cooper?"

Huh?

The dirty words flowing out of his mouth and the heat in his eyes made it hard to even think. Then there was the hand that kept rubbing the cheek he'd smacked. Soothing the skin or teasing me, the results were the same. I was just about panting; the sensation felt so incredible.

"What are you supposed to be doing, Cooper?" His gravelly voice made my cock jerk.

"Kissing Sawyer. You wanted to see us kiss." Just saying it made it sound dirty. He wanted to watch us together.

"Good boy. But you're still being naughty." His hand came down again, and my head fell back as I moaned. If he kept doing that, I'd never be able to think enough to obey. Maybe that was the point.

Jackson wanted to spank me.

God, could the night get any hotter?

"I think you're going to have to go over my lap. Sawyer,

what do you think? Is our naughty boy in need of a punishment?" His hand came down again twice in rapid succession. Not hard, but enough to make every muscle clench in anticipation.

I couldn't wait to see how it felt when I was naked for Master.

Sawyer was wide-eyed and somewhere between desperately needy and shockingly aroused. Finally, he nodded slowly. "He does. He's been naughty all week, and I don't think he's going to be good for you until he learns his lesson."

It was every fantasy we'd ever talked about together, but somehow even better. People always said that dreams were better than reality when it came to kink and BDSM, but I thought that meant they'd done it wrong. Because Jackson's touch and his commanding presence were more incredible than I'd imagined they would be.

"Naughty boy." His hand came down again, and it took me a minute to realize what I'd done. *Oops.* "Do you think you get to touch your cock when we're together? Without permission?"

Damn.

Completely insane.

"I'm sorry." I honestly hadn't realized that I'd reached down to touch myself. But the spanking and making out with Sawyer because Jackson wanted to see us, and even the knowledge that everything was finally starting to happen, was too arousing to keep my hands off my cock. "My pants are still on, though."

I wasn't naked and touching it. That had to count for something.

Evidently not.

"No, that doesn't make it better." Jackson's voice made it sound like he was disappointed in me, but his eyes told a different story altogether. They were filled with desire, and I could see all the wonderful things he wanted to do to us in them.

Jackson's hand continued rubbing slow circles over the sensitive skin, and all I wanted was to be free of my clothes because that was going to make it more incredible. "I think you're going to be even harder to control when you're naked. Yes, a good spanking is what you need first."

I just about melted.

I looked at Jackson, peeking through my lashes, and gave him a little pout. "Yes, Master."

He made a low, sexy sound, and Sawyer laughed. "Little tease."

Cocking my head, I gave him a mock frown. "I'm not a tease. I'm totally going to put out."

"After we get some of that sass under control." Jackson's deep voice made me shiver.

"Now?" That came out a little more hopeful than it should have for an actual punishment, but Jackson didn't seem to mind. He grinned and shook his head like I was incredible.

"Yes, now." Then Jackson turned to Sawyer and gave him a tender kiss. "Do you want to help me get him ready for his spanking, or do you just want to watch?"

The longing was clear in Sawyer's eyes, but I wasn't sure what his mouth would say. They had major issues agreeing on anything. If they were a couple, I'd say it was time for counseling. In Sawyer's case, he needed more time.

"I'll help…" There was a little pause or maybe it just felt that way to me. I knew what he wanted to call Jackson…Master. He just couldn't believe that we actually found him. I knew he would get there, eventually.

"I'm glad." Sawyer got another sweet kiss. "But if it's too much, what do you do?"

Sawyer smiled like Jackson was the cutest thing ever. "Safeword and let you know."

"Thank you." Jackson gave Sawyer a kiss on his forehead. Then smacked my ass. "Bedroom?"

"Yes!" Spanking and sex. That was what I wanted so badly I could taste it. And as hot as it was watching Sawyer and Jackson kiss on the couch, if we tried to have sex on it, someone was going to end up falling off.

Not sexy at all.

They both grinned wickedly like they knew exactly what they were going to do to me. They were so sexy and so cute. I wasn't going to deny I was excited about the sex. Because it was going to be off-the-charts hot, I just knew it.

But the look of trust and the emotions that were starting to grow behind the sexy smile on Sawyer's face made me want to hug him and tell him everything would be fine. But he needed to see it for himself. He was beginning to take the first steps, though. Just the fact that he was right there with us and making out with Jackson was a wonderful start.

And not just because it was hot.

For Sawyer, letting someone in to see the submission and the fantasies that he shared with me meant he was starting to trust them. Before he left home, it was different. He was freer with his feelings, and from the way his stories made it sound, he even hinted at his submissive feelings with some of the guys he'd slept with.

After we left, things changed.

I don't know if it was the pressure he was under or a combination of everything that went on, but it made him more reserved. To see him letting Jackson lead and hearing that they'd at least talked about submission was enough. That they'd brought up safewords was beautiful. I wanted him happy, and I knew Jackson could help give him what I couldn't.

Untangling the mess of arms and legs, we finally got off the couch and started for the bedroom. I got another *no* from Jackson when I started stripping off my clothes, and then another smack on my ass when I pouted about the *no*.

Perfect.

By the time we'd crossed the apartment and entered the bedroom, I was a mess. My cock was so hard it hurt, and it was rubbing against my jeans. I wanted to be naked and over his lap, but Jackson was hell-bent on taking his time.

Jackson gave both of us tender kisses and stepped back, leaving us in the center of the room. Toeing off his shoes, he looked at Sawyer. "I want you to take off his clothes. Slowly, though. I want to enjoy seeing you strip him down."

We both moaned.

My hands were shaking so badly; I was glad I wasn't going to have to work the buttons on my jeans. There was nothing more ridiculous than having to ask for help getting your clothes off when you were supposed to be sexy.

Strippers did not stop midshow and ask someone to help them undo their pants because they'd thought the button-fly jeans were sexy and didn't realize getting them off when they were horny would be difficult. I learned that lesson the hard way. No more button-fly for me.

Watching Jackson climb up on our bed, looking just as sexy as I'd imagined he would, I jumped when I felt Sawyer's fingers tease at the edge of my shirt. His voice was low and sexy, but I could hear the humor in it. "Someone's very excited."

Nodding frantically, I stared at Jackson as he leaned back on the pillows, propped up like a sex god who was letting his subjects entertain him. He was always so laid-back and relaxed with us that the new side of him was magnetic and just pulled me in. I wanted to see what else his new side would think of.

"Draw his shirt up slowly. I want you to unwrap my present carefully, so we don't rush." The low voice was sexy, but Jackson made it sound like Sawyer was opening a present at Christmas, and not a person.

It was crazy hot.

"Raise your arms." Sawyer's low command wasn't the same Dom tone he used when we were playing; it was a sub following his master's orders. I could almost hear different words in my head....*Raise your arms for Master.*

I knew it was what he wanted to say. He just wasn't ready to cross that line yet.

My arms sprang up so fast they both gave low chuckles that sent shivers down my spine. They were trying to torture me, but if it was a punishment, it was the most ingenious thing they could have thought of.

As the shirt inched up, Jackson's gaze got even hotter, and his legs spread apart just enough that I knew how hard he had to be. When the shirt was finally off and tossed to the floor, Sawyer let his hands trail down my arms and around to my chest. His fingers brushed over me with the lightest touch.

He was being careful with Master's present.

When I thought he was finally going to take off my pants, Jackson stopped him. "Not yet. Go back up and show me how sensitive his nipples are. I want to see you play with him. I liked watching my boys kiss."

We both moaned. Knowing he was watching and that we were both submitting to what he wanted was amazing. Sawyer slowly worked his way back up my abs and chest, and I could feel Jackson's gaze following Sawyer's hands.

A light touch circled my nipples, getting closer but making me wait with each pass around the sensitive skin. I loved having them played with. They were small and dark against my pale skin. I'd been so skinny and short as a teenager; standing in front of someone like this would have been embarrassing. But though I hadn't grown much taller as I'd gotten older, I'd filled out enough that muscles corded my chest, and I even had pretty sexy abs.

I'd never look porn-star hot, but it was easy to see Jackson's appreciation for my body.

Just as Sawyer's fingers were about to finally caress my nipples, Jackson stopped him again. "Wait, Sawyer. Does he like it when you play with them hard or does a light touch make him beg?"

"Hard!" It wasn't my question, but the word just popped out.

"Naughty boy. Was it your turn to talk? Presents are supposed to look pretty for their masters, not demand things."

Naughty meant more punishment, right?

"I'm sorry, Master." I knew I was supposed to apologize, but all I really wanted to do was beg for my punishment to start. The wait was almost painful.

Jackson shook his head like he didn't believe me at all and focused his gaze on Sawyer. "Start off slow. Then I want you to work those little nubs hard. I want to see how prettily he begs for more. I bet you can make some wonderful sounds come out of my present."

We both moaned again in unison, and Jackson smiled wickedly.

"Play with my present, Sawyer."

Damn.

Sawyer did as Master told him to. His fingers flicked over the sensitive peaks and the careful, light pleasure was almost painful. I needed so much more than the gentle touch that was circling my nipples.

I tried to be good.

I tried to let it build so Master could watch.

I broke.

"Please, God, fuck, please do it harder, Master. Please let him do it harder." I think we all knew I couldn't control myself enough to last. It was just too difficult.

"Naughty boy." *God, that was hot.* "Don't let my present rush you, Sawyer."

I might have whimpered, but Jackson gave a low chuckle. Sawyer's slow teasing touch continued until I was panting and making little needy sounds. Master's present was going to explode if they didn't pinch its nipples.

"Please!"

Jackson must have given some kind of signal that I missed, because from one second to the next, the careful touch turned to rough and incredible. Lightning shot through me, and I cried out at the flood of sensation. Leaning into Sawyer's warmth, I closed my eyes and let the pleasure wash over me.

I gave up trying to keep track of how long it lasted. Sometimes Jackson's voice called out to slow down, and other times he talked about "playing rougher with his present." When Sawyer's hands finally started moving down my chest again, the loss was almost painful.

I needed more.

It was hard to focus as I opened my eyes and looked at Master. I was shaky and though we hadn't done much, I felt like I'd run a marathon. Jackson's heated gaze was focused entirely on Sawyer's hand as it opened the buttons and freed my erection.

At Jackson's order, Sawyer finally pushed my pants down, and I stepped out as they puddled around my feet, grateful that I'd already stripped my shoes and socks off as I came in the front door. The briefs caught Jackson's eye, and he smiled wickedly. Tiny and black, they cupped my erection beautifully, and I knew if he caught a look at them from the back, he'd like them even better.

Sawyer called them "fuck me" underwear.

"Do you want to unwrap the last part of your present?" Sawyer's words were quiet and needy, but it sounded different. Had he finally accepted what I'd known right away? Was it something else? I was desperate for him to understand, so it was probably just me.

I wanted him happy.

I wanted him to have the family we'd dreamed of.

And I wanted to come.

Jackson's husky voice made me whimper. "Yes, Sawyer, thank you. And he still needs his spanking."

I was going to explode. *Bam.* And then there would be naked sub splattered all over the walls.

I felt Sawyer lean close and kiss my cheek. He stepped closer, and I automatically moved forward following the unsaid instructions. As he straightened, I heard him whisper too low for Jackson to hear, "Go to Master, Coop. He needs you."

He needed us both. But I'd correct Sawyer when I had more blood in my brain.

Sawyer led me across the room and helped me up onto the bed and into Jackson's arms. I worried for a moment when he stepped away, but when he climbed onto the mattress and sat at Jackson's feet I relaxed.

"Over my lap for your spanking. I can feel you shivering like one of the excited little dogs in my classes. You just need someone to take you in hand, and you'll feel so good. Some discipline to go with all that love you get from Sawyer." Jackson's words were low and tender as he laid me over his lap, so I was stretched out across the bed. "Come here, Sawyer, help me get him ready."

I was too excited to see what Jackson did, but I felt the bed move and then Sawyer's body by my legs. Pressing my face into the mattress, I whimpered and tried not to grind my desperately hard cock into Jackson's rock-hard thighs. The wait was excruciating.

Careful fingers that I knew were Sawyer's eased the briefs over my ass and let them catch just below my cheeks. I wanted them off, but all they did was wrap my cock tighter in the fabric and make it harder to think.

I was expecting more of the same slow, painful build up, but Jackson's hand came down quickly, and the smack echoed in the room. A startled sound burst out of me, but the pure pleasure that radiated up my spine had me moaning and arching up for more.

"Naughty boy. Driving everyone crazy this week. Teasing us and telling me such wicked things. You like getting us turned-on and desperate, don't you, sassy boy?" The words were rough, but the erotic need and arousal that pulsed through them only made them sexier.

"I'll be good." I'd try. It was a white lie.

"I'm sorry, Master." Another little lie. I was going to love every minute of making them both insane, and every minute of the punishment that would hopefully follow.

His hand came down over and over, slowly letting the heat build. When he stopped, it was too soon. I needed more. But before I could start to beg, he spoke to Sawyer. "Lean down and give that sexy pink bottom a kiss. I can see how you're looking at it. Let me see how you want to touch him, Sawyer."

Sawyer gave a desperate little sound, and then I felt the bed move and his lips touch my ass. He peppered my sensitive skin with kisses and little flicks of his tongue. It made everything inside me start to boil, and I thrust my cock against Jackson's legs.

"Oh, I don't think he's learned his lesson yet, Sawyer."

Sawyer's mouth left my skin, and Jackson's hand came down again. The perfect torture continued over and over. The kisses and almost innocent exploration of his mouth, and then the pain when I finally gave in to the demanding urge to move.

I lost track of how long it went on. When the measured swats slowed, I expected the kisses to start again, but Jackson had something else in mind. "I think you want to kiss something else, don't you, Sawyer?"

Sawyer gave a low sound, but my brain wasn't working enough to figure out what it meant. When Jackson's strong grip spread my cheeks, I finally understood. Whimpers and begging sounds burst out as I felt Sawyer's tongue circle my hole.

He licked and teased and kissed, and when I cried out, his tongue pushed inside me like he was shallowly fucking me. Jackson gripped my ass tighter, and the combination was too much. The pain and the wicked pleasure sent me over the edge before I could even find the words to say something.

Shaking and bucking into Jackson's tight grip, the waves of pleasure rolled over me as I rutted against his thighs. Sawyer's tongue kept teasing me, and I could hear his moans as he kept pushing the climax higher and longer.

When it finally slowed, and I flopped down over Jackson's legs, I felt both their hands rubbing over me in long soothing strokes. All I could manage to move was my head, so I turned and looked at my two loves. "I'm sorry. I was naughty."

Jackson knew right away what I meant. "You didn't have permission to come, did you?"

"No." But God, it'd been fabulous.

"I'll just have to keep punishing you again later until you understand the rules."

Nodding, I gave him a lazy smile. "Later."

His hand rubbed over my ass, and he chuckled quietly. "A few days, I think. Then another punishment for my boy."

That sounded perfect. But in that moment, I just wanted to curl up and cuddle. Spanking could wait. For a while at least.

It took too long to realize that they hadn't come. Jackson effortlessly lifted me off his legs and moved me, so I was resting beside him on the pillows, curled tight to his body. Before I could say anything, Jackson turned to Sawyer and pulled him, so he was lying stretched out over Jackson.

"Let me taste him on your lips."

Hottest sentence ever.

16

JACKSON

Sawyer surged into me, and I could feel his cock rub against mine as he leaned in and gave me his lips. He didn't demand. He didn't control. He simply offered himself up to me. He was beautiful and sweet, and I had no idea how far he wanted to go.

It was maddening.

I wanted it to be perfect for both of them, but I wasn't sure what he needed. Well, I thought I knew, but he was so much more careful than Cooper was with what he said and how he expressed what he was feeling. I was a bit lost without the constant stream of sexy desperation that poured from Cooper. I needed to give Sawyer everything he wanted, but I wasn't sure he knew what that was.

Cooper made quiet, needy noises as he watched us kiss, and I felt his hand snake between us and ease under my shirt, so he could caress my chest. My kissing Sawyer after he'd been playing with Cooper's tight little hole made Cooper insanely turned-on. My dirty boy loved it. So did Sawyer if the feel of his hard dick was any indication.

I let my hands roam over his back and down to cup his ass.

That'd clearly been okay earlier, so I wasn't as concerned. He moaned louder and opened up even more for me, a clear signal for me to keep going. I just had to keep reminding myself that he had his safeword and trust that he would use it.

After everything that we'd done, and his reaction to Cooper's spanking, I was reasonably confident I could get him off with something like that. Kneading his muscular ass and occasionally letting my fingers tease over his hole was making him crazy. Playing with his ass also let me control the speed of his thrust as he ground his cock against mine.

Every muscle was tight, but the way he was pressed against me, and the desperate little noises he was making screamed out his submission louder than anything else he could have done. When I broke away from his mouth and started kissing down his neck, he offered it up to me, and pleas started tumbling out of him.

"Please, I need. I have to. Please." Master didn't come out, but I could almost hear it floating between us. It wasn't the word that really mattered, but I knew to Sawyer, the word would mean something.

It would be his way of accepting what was happening between us.

"Do you want to come, Sawyer? Do you want to keep rubbing off against me or do you want me to free that sexy trapped cock of yours, so you can feel my hand on it? So you can feel my fingers wrapped around it while you explode? You've been such a good boy this week, I'm going to let you choose this time." I don't know if it was the good boy or if it was the idea of what might happen the next time we were together, but he started nodding and trying to make his hands work enough to start stripping off his clothes.

I wasn't so much worried about me getting off as I was making sure they had an incredible experience, so I was perfectly happy with the way the night was going. Cooper, on the other hand, had a different idea.

The little tease sat up and started sprinkling kisses over Sawyer and I. Cheeks, lips, noses, anything he could reach. "But then you're going to fuck me, right, Master? I haven't felt you inside me yet, and Sawyer didn't even fuck me this morning. I need you, Master."

Cooper's words were dirty and needy and beautiful.

Sawyer's eyes widened as we both turned to look at Cooper. He was giving me his best sexy pout, one hand teasing his nipples and the other circling around his hardening cock. If I needed any proof of their age, his response time was it.

I reached around and grabbed one of his cheeks roughly, making sure my fingers caressed the outer edges of his little hole. "You want to feel my cock inside you?" Cooper groaned, and his head fell back.

"Please, Master."

"And you didn't even get to feel Sawyer's hard cock in you this morning? Why not?"

Cooper was starting to thrust his ass back against my hand, and his little wiggles were clearly trying to get my fingers to close the last gap, so I could play with his hole. "Cooper, were you naughty?"

He reluctantly nodded, and Sawyer chuckled. Cooper gave me a pout like he was very sorry. "I woke him up early. I was just so excited for your date."

He was so excited for my date with Sawyer that he couldn't sleep? My sweet pup was so cute. "I'm glad you were excited. And you're right, I think we need to fill your needy hole."

Moving my hand slightly, my fingers caressed over his opening and a shiver ran through him. Tapping and circling the sensitive skin, I turned back to Sawyer, running my free hand over his chest to play with his nipples. "Do you want to help me make love to him and fuck his tight little hole?"

Sawyer gave a low groan, and I could see his mind whirling. But he nodded and leaned in to give me a kiss. "Yes, please."

Pulling my hand away from Cooper's needy body, I smiled at his groan of protest. "Let's get you ready then. You're wearing far too many clothes to help me make love to him."

Sawyer nodded and sat up on his knees, a clear indication of his readiness. Reaching for his pants, I quickly started stripping them off. His muscular body was beautiful no matter what he was wearing, but naked took it to a whole new level.

My hands itched to roam over his skin, and as I pushed the pants and briefs over his ass and full erection, I let them play. He blushed and shivered but let my hands explore his body and even pressed back into them when I reached around to grab his ass.

His lids dropped halfway, and his head fell back when I finally brought my fingers around to caress over his hips and at the sensitive juncture where his leg met his body. By the time I took his cock in my hand, he was breathing heavily, and it was clear to see he was racing toward his orgasm.

"We need to get Cooper ready if we're going to fill that sexy ass of his. You've been such a good boy this week, I'm going to watch you sink that beautiful cock of yours into him."

Cooper gave a needy little sound that had us both turning to him. "And you too?"

He couldn't seem to understand how it was going to work, and I had to smile. "Yes, we're going to put you here between us, and we're going to take turns filling you up."

A shiver raced through him, and his cock jerked. Someone liked that idea. I reached back and gave his ass a pat. "Over my lap so we can get you ready."

Cooper threw himself across my lap and arched his ass up. No hesitation and no second-guessing. Sawyer smiled and reached over to open the nightstand drawer where I saw lube and an unopened box of condoms.

It could only be Cooper's idea.

Our sexy boy shivered as he heard the lube open, and Sawyer squeezed some out. Then he moaned at the first touch of my finger as I carefully pressed in. Cooper knew exactly what he wanted. He opened up beautifully, and his entire body seemed to relax into my touch.

Sinking into his tight heat, I knew it wouldn't be long before he was ready for more. Sawyer's earlier touch and the orgasm he'd already had made Cooper eager and needy. Looking at my naked sexy Sawyer, I glanced down at Cooper's tight body where it was swallowing up my finger.

"Help me stretch our boy." Sawyer swallowed hard and nodded, slicking up one finger before bringing it to Cooper's opening. "Slide it in right beside mine."

Cooper let out a low guttural moan as Sawyer eased in. We fucked him slowly, carefully stretching him out until he started thrusting back and begging for more. "One more, Sawyer. I want him nice and ready for us."

Running my free hand up and down Cooper's back, I could feel him shake as Sawyer's second one entered him gently. Every time Cooper seemed close to coming, Sawyer instinctively slowed down, keeping him on the edge.

By the time I knew he was ready, more than ready really, his legs didn't work, and Sawyer had to almost hold him up. Cooper found his words, though. "You're going to get naked now, right?"

"Do you want to see me naked?" I wasn't really worried about how I'd look. Great genes and an active lifestyle kept me fit, and a couple of sessions a week at the gym kept me in good shape.

Both boys' heads went up and down like little dolls, and I had to smile. "Help me take them off then."

They made quick work of taking off my clothes. Hands touched and caressed as they stripped everything away. Cooper explored my chest and teased at my nipples, and drawing sounds of pleasure from me seemed to be the game. Sawyer sat up and grabbed the lube that had fallen on the bed and brought his slick hand to my cock.

"We need to get you ready." He hid his wicked side deeper than Cooper, but I could see how much he loved being able to touch and tease me.

"You too. I can't wait to see you slide deep inside our boy." Slicking up my fingers, I explored his cock while he gave me the same pleasure.

When we were both ready—my condom was on, we were both slicked up, and Cooper was so frantic I thought he'd end up shattering at the first thrust—I reached for my excitable boy and moved him to straddle my legs. We both moaned when Sawyer took my cock and held it steady at Cooper's readied opening.

Sliding him down slowly, I felt his body stretch around me, and his head fell back as he groaned low and needy. Sawyer's hands came around to tease at Cooper's still-sensitive peaks, and soon we had Cooper writhing on my cock.

When he was completely filled, and I could feel his body clenching around my shaft, I reached around and gave his ass a little tap. "Let me see you ride my cock. Show us how much you want to be fucked."

Wonderful little sounds escaped him as he started to ride me. He had a way of moving that always drew everyone's eye, but when the pleasure was running through him, it was even sexier. A combination of grace and pure excitement, I couldn't help but watch the desire flowing through him.

He felt incredible around me, and it was all I could do to keep from rolling over and fucking him senseless. When I grabbed his hips and stopped the perfection that was running through both of us, he started to whine.

"I want to see Sawyer fuck you now."

That stopped the protest before it'd even started. As my cock slipped out of him, he arched back and offered his body to Sawyer. It wasn't the right angle to see Sawyer actually enter him, but I could see the minute he breached Cooper, because the pleasure rolled off both of them in waves.

They were perfect together.

They'd explored each other for years, and their love rolled off each other. I should have felt excluded, like an outsider watching, but somehow they pulled me in. I could feel their emotions wrapping around me, and I knew they were making me part of their family.

After a few minutes, Sawyer pulled out leaving Cooper aching and empty again. He leaned in close and whispered low to Cooper. "It's Master's turn to fuck you now."

It wasn't exactly calling me Master, but it was beautiful coming from his mouth. Cooper thought so too, because a smile broke out over his face. "Yes, please, I need more. Please."

The tension continued to build as we took turns filling Cooper. Every time he got close enough to come, we would switch, and it would pull him back just enough to keep him on edge. He was incredible. When Sawyer was buried deep in him again, I reached around and started teasing at Sawyer's nipples and letting my fingers caress along his hips.

Something inside him shattered. At first, I'd thought he'd come, but he stilled instead and looked at me. Stretching up, I pressed Cooper between us and took Sawyer's lips in a tender kiss. It was sweet and filled with emotion though we were all naked, and Cooper was writhing on his cock.

Pulling back, I cupped his face. "What do you need, Sawyer? Just tell me."

Some of the turmoil I could feel running through him faded, and he gave me a loving look. "You. I want you, Master."

An excited shiver ran through Cooper, but I held him still while I watched Sawyer closely. They were so different, but each needed so much. I thought I knew what he was asking, but I wanted to be sure. "Do you want me to make love to you too?"

He nodded and leaned in to ask for another kiss. Giving him one, that time filled with heat and passion, I pulled back. "Of course. I would love that." I knew right away how it needed to work. "Cooper, on your hands and knees. I want you to offer up that sexy ass for Sawyer."

A nearly frantic Cooper threw himself down on the bed, head low and ass up in need. Sex hadn't been something funny for me in the past, but I couldn't help smiling as I watched my boy. Turning to Sawyer, I gave him a tender kiss. "All right, Sawyer, get behind him."

I watched for any sign that Sawyer had changed his mind, but there wasn't any fear or indecision. He looked nervous, but the heated looks he gave Cooper and me spelled out just how much he wanted it.

From everything they'd both said, I knew Sawyer was desperate to give up the more dominant role he'd given himself in their relationship. Even though topping during sex was something they took turns at, it wasn't an instinctual Dom response for him. The weight of everything had to be heavy on his shoulders.

There wasn't a lot I could do in other areas of their life yet; it was too new. But this was something I could give him. I could help the tender, caring man who just wanted to give Cooper everything he could a chance to turn everything off and sink into the bliss of knowing there wasn't anything he had to decide, and nothing was up to him.

Stripping off the used condom and putting it in the trash by the bed, I grabbed the lube from where it had fallen to the end of the mattress and I moved behind Sawyer. Tossing it to the side, I ran my hands up and down his back, soothing, but hopefully letting him know how beautiful he was. "That's right."

Finally reaching around him, I gripped Cooper's hip in one

hand and Sawyer's cock with the other. He was long and thick, and so hard I could almost feel the blood pumping through it. "I'm going to use this cock to fuck Cooper. Do you understand, Sawyer? This is my toy, and I'm using it to play with my present."

Sawyer sagged against me, his back resting against my chest as his hard cock pulsed in my hand. "Yes, Master."

"My strong, beautiful boy, there's nothing to decide. There's nothing you need to do but listen to me and let me play with my toy. Do you understand?" *Please let him understand.*

He gave me a slow nod, tilting his head so it rested on my shoulder. "You're in charge."

"I'm going to fill you up and show you how a good boy gets rewarded. You want that, don't you? I'm going to watch my boys explode and feel you come around my cock. I'm going to see how incredible you look when I'm using your cock to fuck Cooper. Do you see how he wants it? He's shaking, and any minute he's going to push back and try to fuck himself on my toy. Isn't that right, naughty boy?"

"I'll be good. Please let him fuck me. I'll be good." Cooper cried the words out over and over, desperate and at the end of his rope.

Sawyer's hips gave a jerk, and his dick kissed the clenched hole that quivered in front of it. "That's right. I want you to slide in, but you can't move yet. You've been such a good boy, but I need to get you ready."

I shifted my weight and pushed against Sawyer just enough that his cock started sinking into Cooper. My naughty little thing was so close to his orgasm, he made desperate little sounds, begging for more, but I wasn't ready to give him more.

Not yet, at least.

When Sawyer was fully seated in Cooper's ass, I gave Cooper's hip one last squeeze and moved both hands to grip Sawyer's firm cheeks. "Beautiful boy. Look how sexy you look.

Now don't move....You're going to stay still. If you start moving, he might come, and then I'd have to punish you. You don't want me to have to punish you, do you?"

Sawyer shook his head, everything in him focused on his dick and Cooper's tight body wrapped around it. Cooper, however, loved the idea, and it only sent him higher. "Yes, punish him. I want to see how it looks. He's so sexy like that. Please punish him."

I had to chuckle at the flood of words that cascaded from Cooper. He knew exactly what he wanted. Everything. Every touch. Every punishment. Every kiss. And he wanted to watch it all too—as it happened again to Sawyer. "Naughty boy."

I reached back around and squeezed down on his still-pink bottom. He made a low mewling sound and must have clenched down on Sawyer, because Sawyer's whole body shook and his eyes clamped shut.

It was beautiful. "He feels so good wrapped around you. But you can't make him come."

"I won't. I'll be good." The quiet words were firm and sure.

"I know you will. Because you know you need to have permission to come." It wasn't a question, but he nodded anyway, desperately holding on to his willpower.

I reached down and grabbed the lube, then found the condoms. They both moaned as the top snapped open. The sound was unmistakable, and as my hand rubbed against Sawyer's ass, his breathing sped up and little shivers raced through him.

When I finally circled his hole with one slick finger, he made a low cry, and his body opened up, nearly pulling me in. He was tight, but he knew what he wanted, and he knew how incredible it was going to feel. Carefully fucking him with one finger, I smiled wickedly when I found his prostate.

Desperate sounds escaped, and his hands reached back to grab at me, but he never moved his cock. It stayed right where

I'd put it. "Cooper, he's so tight and perfect. He's going to feel so good wrapped around me."

They both made sexy low noises, and I chuckled. God, they were incredible. Sawyer was quickly ready for two fingers, and as much as I loved teasing them, poor Sawyer had been hard for ages, and Cooper was at the end of his rope, though he'd already gotten to come.

When he took three fingers easily, I pulled them out and gripped his hips, pressing my cock against his body. "Are you ready, Sawyer? Are you ready for me to fuck Cooper with your dick?"

Cooper cried out a frantic, "Yes, he is!"

A broken sound escaped Sawyer, half laugh and half sob, as I put on the new condom and slicked it up with the remaining lube. He nodded, and his hands frantically tugged at me. "Please, yes. Please, yes."

I surged into him.

Every thrust made them both cry out as Sawyer's cock pushed deeper into Cooper. The tight grip I had on Sawyer's hips let me set the pace, but it was clear neither of them could wait. Cooper's frantic cries only made Sawyer's need worse, and his body started to clench around me as he raced toward his orgasm.

"My sweet, special boys." Kissing down Sawyer's neck, I tried to make both boys understand how wonderful they were. "Come for me."

When Cooper finally broke, his orgasm forced Sawyer's as well. They both cried out, only seconds apart, and the rhythmic clenching of Sawyer's body was too much to resist. One last thrust, and I finally gave in to the orgasm that had been pulling at me for what felt like days.

Fucking them both through the pleasure, I kept going until I saw Cooper fall to the bed, spent and finally exhausted. My little Energizer Bunny. Well...pup.

Sawyer leaned back until I was sitting on the bed, and he was still impaled on my cock, almost curled up on my lap. It gave me wicked ideas for pleasing my boys next time, but for now, I wrapped my arms around him and held him tight as my cock softened inside him.

Running my hands over his body, I finally laid him down next to Cooper. Quickly taking care of the condom in the trashcan by the bed, I lay back down next to them. Cooper gave a low frustrated huff, and with uncoordinated movements climbed over both Sawyer and me.

"You're supposed to be in the middle."

"Is that how this works?" I tried not to laugh, but my sleepy pup was too cute.

"Duh." His sarcastic tone got him another pop on his ass, which had him melting into me. "Oh, more please, Master."

Laughing, Sawyer shifted so he could lay his head on my chest and wrap his body around one side. "Don't get him going again."

Cooper stuck his tongue out, but I could see the joy in his eyes. Wrapping my arms around them both, I shook my head. "Come here."

Both yawning, they cuddled closer. Cooper's hand started absently caressing my chest. "You have to stay."

It wasn't a question, but I felt the need to respond, anyway. "If that's what you both want."

They nodded in unison, and I let my fingers caress and soothe my tired boys. I hadn't planned on staying over, but there was nowhere else I wanted to be. Sandwiched between the two men who were coming to mean so much to me, it was perfect.

"I think my cake is still on the table, and we need a bigger bed. My ass is hanging off." Cooper grumbled into my chest.

Okay, almost perfect.

"Well, we can't have that. You know, I have a king-sized bed at my house and a shower big enough for all of us." And a few toys that might be fun to play with as well.

The internet was a wonderful place.

Cooper jerked his head in what I thought was supposed to be a nod. I smiled. "Sleepy boy, you said you needed a shower."

He grumbled about his cake and tried to wiggle closer, but that must have made it even more evident *why* he needed a shower. The cum dripping out of his well-loved hole was sexy, but not something he wanted to go to sleep with.

"Just a few more minutes." I felt him press a kiss to my chest, and one hand reached over to grab Sawyer's. Watching the two boys share the tender moment with me made my heart swell.

"All right, sweet boy. A few more minutes."

Sawyer's reply was low and filled with emotion. "I think you'll be here for longer than that."

"You're right. I'm not going anywhere."

17

SAWYER

"Are you sure this is going to be okay?" Making yet another left turn that didn't make me feel we were heading in the correct direction, I glanced over at Cooper as I followed the drone of the GPS. "And are you sure you put in the right address?"

"Yes." Cooper sighed and looked down at the phone. "We're on the other side of that strip mall that has the bakery and the adult toy store. It's just over that way." He gestured toward the woods, flicking his hands in several directions at once.

"What do you mean we're behind the mall? We've been driving for like twenty minutes." What the hell was he talking about?

He shrugged and gave me a look like I was being ridiculous. "That last road we passed was the one that goes behind the mall."

"Then why have I been driving around in circles with this damned GPS when you knew where we were going? And why the hell does your phone sound British?" I knew I was overreacting, but I couldn't seem to help it.

He gave me a look like I couldn't get any more stupid. "Because it's sexier than the regular one."

It was the silent *Duh* that made me lose it. "It's impossible to understand!"

"You're just nervous. Don't go all Godzilla on me. I'm not China." His sassy retort made me insane.

"That movie wasn't set in China! How many times do I have to remind you of that!"

"Oh, look, there it is." Cooper ignored me completely and pointed out the small sign I must have somehow missed three times.

Pulling into the driveway that led to Jackson's house and his business, I followed the directions he gave us and kept going back around the edge of the property. As I parked beside his truck, I took a deep breath and turned off the car.

"You've been driving me crazy on purpose."

"Yup. But I'd rather have you going all Godzilla on me than worrying." Leaning over to give me a quick kiss, he grinned and jumped out of the car.

"Jackson! We're here!"

Cooper nearly danced across the driveway, bouncing and calling out. The little nuisance. I might love him, but I was seriously thinking about getting him a muzzle and never letting him control the GPS again. Closing my eyes, I tried to relax as the front door opened and voices talked excitedly.

I could hear Jackson getting closer to Cooper's open car door. "What did you do to Sawyer?"

Cooper was quiet, so he must have shrugged, but then he sighed dramatically and started talking in a mock-whisper. "I'd rather have him grumpy than worried."

"What's he worried about?"

"I'm not supposed to tell, but since you asked, he can't complain." I could almost hear the excited smile in Cooper's voice. "I have my puppy stuff in the back of the car. You said you were curious."

"And I said that we'd talk about it later with him because you weren't supposed to ambush him with it." I couldn't resist hollering out.

It was quiet for a moment, and then Cooper's door shut and mine opened. Turning my head, I opened one eye. Thankfully, for Cooper's sake, it was Jackson. "Hi."

"Hi." One of his strong hands came up to cup my face, and I closed my eyes, sinking into his warmth. He let me relax for a moment as his fingers gently caressed my skin, then started talking again. "What happened?"

"He pretended to be confused and did something to the GPS so it would send us in circles. He knew exactly where this was."

Jackson coughed, covering a laugh. *Traitor.* "He texted me about half an hour ago and said you guys were going to be late."

"Nope. Not until he started driving me crazy."

"Why was he driving you crazy? Were you worried about the things he has in the trunk, or is it something else?"

"That. He said you were curious, but it seems too soon to start forcing you into that part of our lives."

"Too soon for you, or too soon for Cooper? Because I have to say, if we make him wait too many more weeks, I think I'm going to wake up to a naked pup in my house as a surprise."

I could hear the smile in his voice, but he was right. It was something Cooper would do. "For me." I took another breath. "Are you disappointed that I'm not there yet?"

"Absolutely not." His free hand took one of mine in a firm grip. "We do things at our own pace. Am I completely ready? I'm not sure. Do I love the idea of Cooper showing me a part of himself that makes him so excited and happy it's all he can think about? Yes. So that makes it easier." His thumb started rubbing circles on the back of my hand, and the light touch seemed magnified.

"And I have you to help show me the way. To me, it would be harder if both of you were pups right away. So in a sense, you're doing me a favor." It sounded like Cooper logic, so for a moment, I wondered if Cooper had already given him a very similar speech.

"I know you're starting to trust that I'll be here for you two, and I know you're starting to see me as part of your family. I don't need *us* to rush into something just because Cooper is on his own path."

"It feels a little like Cooper is dragging you along too, no matter if you're ready or not."

"No, he's just enthusiastically calling after me on the trail. So sometimes I hurry up to meet him because it's impossible not to respond to all that happiness and excitement." Jackson leaned in close and kissed me softly. "Come inside. We'll have dinner, and then pick out a movie—easy evening in. Then if we're ready, you can show me Cooper's pup."

Opening my eyes, I looked at Jackson. "And you won't let him rush you? I'd feel terrible if it was too much for you."

"I promise." The hand that was cradling my face pulled me in for another kiss before he stood up. "Come on. Let's see what he thinks of the house."

"He's probably Facebook stalked every picture you've ever posted about it and walked around on Google Earth." I smiled as I got out of the car.

"That would not surprise me." Jackson stepped back and let me close the door, then pulled me into his embrace. "You doing better?"

"Yes." I curled into him and let him wrap his arms around me. "That doesn't mean I won't kill him for making us go around in circles."

Jackson laughed. "I think he was just trying to give you time to relax or something else to focus on."

"That does *not* make it better." It kind of did. But he was going to owe me.

Stepping back, I took Jackson's hand and told myself it was time to fake being an adult. "This is really beautiful."

He shook his head. "Nope, not going to pretend to be okay." Pulling me back into his arms, he held me tight. "Look at me."

It was a bit of an awkward angle, but I followed his instructions.

It wasn't quite the same tone he'd used in bed the other night, but it was close enough that I wanted to do whatever he said. When he had my attention, he nodded. "I'm going to make the decision about the puppy-play time later. I might let Cooper show me his pup, or I might explain to him that we're going to do it another time. Either way, I will not make you show me anything until you're ready. However, since Cooper is ready, I'm going to take charge of that for him. Do you understand?"

Nodding, relief flooded through me. If Jackson was comfortable enough to be Cooper's master not just in bed but also during playtime, I knew he had to be somewhat okay with it. I didn't want the excitement to push him into something he wasn't ready for. I didn't want to chase him away. It was a lot to handle, and Cooper didn't always realize that.

"Yes, Sir."

Jackson's smile grew more heated, and I felt his hands move down my back to my ass. "I love hearing you say that." Then leaning close, he took my mouth in a long, passionate kiss. The tenderness and love he always projected was still there, but the kiss wasn't about comfort or soothing my nerves; it was about claiming me.

When he finally pulled back, he gave me a long look. "As Master, I'm going to be taking more control, do you understand that?"

"Yes, Master." It was freeing, and just the word was beautiful.

"Good boy. The first thing I'm taking control of is my pup in there." His hands squeezed down on my cheeks. "But we're going to talk about more things soon."

Arousal poured off Jackson, but he didn't say what else he was going to control. But the possibilities were incredible and erotic. I couldn't help but ask. "Like what?"

I wanted to know.

I had to know.

I was afraid he was actually going to tell me.

Jackson's heated smile turned wicked, and he leaned down to kiss my neck. Working his way down from my ear, he whispered low. "I might control your orgasms. I might control how you get to make love to Cooper even when I'm not around. I might even control when you get hard. I've found the most interesting toys online to help remind subs who they belong to. And the most fascinating things for pups as well."

Fuck.

Might. Might. Might. His teasing possibilities were going to make me crazy. "When?"

"When I'm ready." He said it so simply. He was Master, and he'd decide how things progressed. The last weight I didn't even realize I was carrying around lifted.

"Yes, Master." God, that was sexy.

"I'm glad you understand." He kissed my forehead. "Now, we're going to go find Cooper."

Taking my hand, he started leading me toward the house. It was bigger than I'd expected. He'd mentioned that he'd had it built once the business had taken off, but I pictured something smaller. Something that said bachelor pad.

This screamed family.

The large front porch wrapped around the one-story house and seemed to go down one side as well as toward the back.

With a grayish siding and bright white accents, it looked fancier than anything either of us ever lived in.

Climbing the steps, I wasn't surprised to see Cooper pop out the front door. "He's right. The shower is big enough for all of us—the tub too, probably."

Laughing, I shook my head. "Snoop."

"Nope. He said to make myself at home. How could I make myself at home if I didn't know what was in it? See?"

Cooper logic.

"You know that wasn't what he meant."

"But it was what he expected would happen." Jackson's hand came down and smacked my ass lightly. It wasn't even painful, but sensation flooded through me. "No arguing."

"Yes, Master." Our voices blended together, mine more serious, and Cooper's clearly lying. He'd talked about getting spanked again for days. He wasn't really worried about behaving.

Jackson didn't seem to believe Cooper either, but he smiled at him anyway. "I didn't even get a kiss from you. You jumped out of the car after being naughty, and then headed right in. I think we need to fix that."

Cooper almost jumped into Jackson's arms. The strong, laughing man just caught him up, so Cooper wrapped his legs around him like a monkey. Giving Jackson a heated kiss, Cooper writhed in his arms, clearly rubbing his cock against Jackson's firm abs.

Jackson chuckled against Cooper's mouth and smacked his ass. Mumbling, "Naughty boy," Jackson went back to taking his mouth, clearly intent on showing Cooper how excited he was as well.

They were both incredible to watch.

I was starting to understand why Cooper liked watching me with Jackson so much. I'd had to hear for days that we needed a mirror in our room, so he could watch Jackson fuck me next time we did it the same way.

He'd made me crazy.

Even though we'd all gone out together on Sunday and they'd had a date Saturday morning, it hadn't been enough for any of us. Phone calls and texts didn't substitute for being held and touched. But it definitely built the anticipation.

Jackson hadn't said anything, but as we'd gotten ready that morning, Cooper and I had both agreed that we weren't going to make love until we saw Jackson. It'd made for a long Friday. But now we both had the evening off, and Cooper didn't even have to go in on Saturday, so the plan was to stay the night and have fun.

We were both pretty sure that was code for have sex until we all passed out.

Or at least, that was what we were hoping.

Cooper couldn't seem to help himself, and Jackson's hand came down again. "Naughty boy."

Pulling back, Jackson smiled at Cooper's manipulative pout. "Let's show Sawyer the house. If you're good, maybe I'll give you another spanking after dinner. But only after you apologize to Sawyer and show him how sorry you are for making him drive in circles."

Cooper only heard sorry and apologize, so his mind went right to sex, and he'd obviously tuned everything else out. He nodded at Jackson's words, but his eyes flew to me, and I knew he was picturing all kinds of naughty, wonderful things.

"I'll show him I'm very sorry, Master." Cooper's voice was breathless and filled with need.

"House, then dinner." Jackson's smile said he knew exactly what Cooper was thinking. "Then apologies."

Jackson reached out to take one of my hands and let the other wrap low around Cooper's waist to play with his ass. It looked like he had plans to make Cooper crazy before he actually got to come.

As he led us through the house, pointing out rooms and showing us around, I had to admit, the house was nicer inside than it was outside. It probably wasn't that big, but the one-story layout made it seem even larger. By the time we'd wandered through every room and Cooper had bounced on Jackson's bed, we were all starving.

"So what's for dinner?" Cooper asked excitedly as he started snooping through kitchen cabinets. "You know you have everything in the wrong place in here. Unloading the dishwasher and putting the stuff away has to take forever. The glasses should be in this one and the plates over here. Not way over there."

"Cooper." Only he would say something like that.

Jackson laughed. "How about you help me rearrange everything one weekend? Show me how it should look."

"Sure." Cooper smiled, completely ignoring my signals to stop it.

"It's not our house."

That got ignored too. By both of them.

Jackson gave him a peck on the lips and started walking over to the fridge. "The guest rooms are kind of empty. I thought that big one would make a good office. But I've never planned out what it should look like."

Not sure how to respond, I watched Jackson move around the room, not caring at all that he'd given Cooper permission to honestly make himself at home. That was supposed to just be an expression.

Jackson set a covered dish on the counter and then placed a plate of vegetables next to it. Cooper looked on, curious. "What's it going to be? We haven't learned to cook much."

Giving Cooper a smile, Jackson pulled back the plastic lid on the glass dish and showed him. "Steaks. I've got the grill heating up, and we're going to cook these as well as some vegetables. I threw some potatoes in the oven earlier, and they should be almost done."

He could cook.

"Sounds wonderful." Cooper gave him a mischievous grin. "What's for dessert?"

Jackson gave him a dirty leer as he picked up the plates. "You."

18

COOPER

"You'll show me how to do that, right?" I looked over the table and leaned forward in the chair. I wasn't exactly stuffed, but it was close. Everything had been delicious.

"How to grill? Of course." Jackson reached out and cupped my face. "I'd love to show you."

Sawyer snorted. "Just make sure you give him good instructions."

Rolling my eyes, I grinned at Jackson and stuck my tongue out at Sawyer. "It was one time. Once you showed me, I never did it again."

Jackson glanced back and forth between us and lifted one eyebrow. Sawyer sighed. "Your excited pup never did laundry at home and never told me after we moved in together. So I sent him down to the laundromat, and he was gone forever. It turned out that he'd gone back and forth from the laundromat to ask the lady who worked at the front desk where we were living how to work the machines and what to do. He was lucky no one stole our stuff."

"I said I'd ask for help the next time I didn't know how to do something." I shrugged. "And she was nice."

Sawyer smiled and nodded. Leaning over, he gave me a kiss. "You did."

Jackson didn't ask the questions I could see behind his eyes, but he smiled and shook his head. "I take it that's part of why you're so honest with each other?"

Sawyer nodded, and my heart squeezed tight. "That's part of it."

Jackson seemed to understand we were turning to more sensitive topics, so he steered the conversation back to the food. "Do you want to come over and practice next weekend? We'll pick a few recipes to try. One for lunch and something else for dinner, maybe? So you get a chance to do it a few times?"

"Yes. We've been cooking more and doing pretty good."

Jackson grinned. "I'm sure you will do wonderful."

"If not, there's always pizza." Sawyer's smile said he wasn't serious. But I still had to react. He was expecting it.

"Like the time you burned the pasta?" I lifted one eyebrow to let him know I wasn't going to let him live that down anytime soon.

Jackson barked out a laugh. "How do you burn pasta?"

Sawyer sighed, and his head dropped back. Giving him a giddy smile, I turned back to Jackson. "Not putting enough water in it, and leaving it there for an hour."

"Hey, there was plenty of water to begin with." He seemed offended, but we'd played it out too many times for me to buy that.

"Of course there was." I was about to make another teasing joke about a mac-n-cheese incident that had gone horribly bad when the back door opened, making us all jump.

A brown-haired woman's head popped around the doorframe. "Should I have knocked?"

She seemed utterly gleeful when she asked, so I knew it had to be his sister. Jackson groaned. "Considering you saw their car, and that's probably the only reason you're here, yes."

"No, it's not. I needed to borrow..." She looked around the room. "Sugar."

He shot her a look like he wanted to throw the sugar at her, not give her some. I liked her already. "Hi, we're...well, I'm Cooper and this is Sawyer....He's, well...we're..."

Once I started, I realized I didn't know how to describe any of it. Finally, I shrugged. "We're having dinner."

She laughed and waggled her eyebrows like a naughty cartoon character. "I know."

"Mellie!"

"Don't give me that stuffed-shirt look. I'm the reason you guys met. Of course I should get to say hi. Especially since everyone's fully clothed and nothing fun's going on." Her eyes lit up when Jackson's head fell back in a fabulous impression of a frustrated Sawyer.

I didn't mind that she knew what we liked and about... well...everything. Sawyer, on the other hand, blushed and looked like he'd rather hide under the table than talk to her about puppy play. Jackson didn't seem to mind any of it. Just the fact that she walked in when she shouldn't have.

But judging by the look on her face, she'd done it on purpose.

He really needed to lock the doors better. We'd have to work on that if I was going to be crawling around the house naked.

Jackson looked at her and shook his head, gesturing to both of us. "As Cooper said, this is Cooper and Sawyer. We're dating, and well on our way to a better label, but we haven't discussed it yet because they weren't ready to be interrogated."

"I'm ready. Sawyer's not." I smiled and waved, but Sawyer threw his napkin at my head.

"I'm Melissa. I'd love to talk to you over coffee sometime. Pick your brain a little if it wouldn't embarrass you." She gave me a wide-eyed, innocent look that was so believable I wanted to tell her anything she wanted to know.

"Mellie!"

I was impressed. She was almost as good as me. "You're good at that."

Melissa didn't seem offended. "Thanks. But you're still going to go out with me, right?"

"Of course." I loved the idea of having someone to talk to who'd understand. "You'll tell me your pen name, right?" I gave her an even better innocent look and nodded encouragingly. "I want to read about your characters. I bet I even have some of your books."

"I love him, Jackie." She beamed at both of us. "Can I keep him?"

"Lord, he's not—fuck, never mind. Just no." Jackson gave her a look like if anyone got to keep me it was going to be him.

They were so funny.

And the fact that he'd been going to tell her that I wasn't a puppy was priceless; even Sawyer had to laugh. She gave him a smile but didn't subject him to the same level of excitement I got, which made me feel even better about hanging out with her. She was trying to drive *Jackie* crazy, but not make us feel weird.

Jackson gave her a frustrated look and ignored our giggling. "Did you actually need something?"

"No. Just wanted to say hi." She waved again, and then started to head out the door. "Cooper, call me. Jackie, give him my number."

Jackson mumbled something under his breath about making her pay for driving him crazy but waved as she left. "Go away. And knock next time!"

She shut the door, laughing.

Sawyer gave Jackson a look and got up to go lock the door. "We've got to talk about you locking the door."

"Agreed." Jackson nodded wholeheartedly. "It wasn't an issue until you guys showed up in my life, though."

"It's an issue now. I'm not getting naked in front of her until I know her a lot better. She's your family and all, not a stranger." I wasn't sure why they both found it so funny, but Sawyer was laughing so hard he almost slid off his chair as he tried to sit down.

"I'll lock the door. I promise." He grinned and stood up. "Help me clear the table and then we can go pick out a movie?"

"Sure. Do I get to choose if I'm good?" I smiled at him and started cleaning up the plates.

"Su—"

"No. You don't know what you're promising. No fair tricking him." Sawyer frowned at me. "He should have full disclosure before he agrees to something like that."

"Spoilsport." Sighing, I kept cleaning up dishes and carrying them to the sink.

Jackson must have given Sawyer a questioning look because Sawyer started to explain. "He has the attention span of a rabbit. He picks something out that he thinks looks good, but then gets bored and starts talking over it or trying to start something naughty. You have to pick the movie that you actually want to see, then he behaves."

Laughing, Jackson started bringing things to the sink. "I think I was almost had."

"I'm being good. Honest." I leaned in and begged for a kiss as he walked past. Stepping close, Jackson gave me a thorough kiss before pulling back, leaving us both breathless.

"Do you want to watch a movie or do something else, my excitable pup?" His heated gaze looked right through me.

"Yes." My response was probably a little too enthusiastic, because he smiled and gave me another kiss before he nodded.

"Okay, go get your bag out of the car and meet me in the living room."

"Naked?"

He groaned a little, and heat flared in his eyes. "Not yet, pup."

"Gotcha." Dancing out of the kitchen as Jackson went to Sawyer, I headed through the house to the front door. Grabbing the keys off the entryway table, I was in and out before Jackson was done helping Sawyer relax, but I figured it would take a few minutes.

Sawyer was worried it would all be too much for Jackson, but he was wrong. Jackson was dying to see me, and I couldn't wait to play with him. By the time they came out of the kitchen, Jackson holding Sawyer's hand, I had everything ready and laid out on the couch.

Pacing around the room to kill time, I couldn't contain my excitement when they walked in. "Now?"

"Yes," Jackson shook his head as I started to strip, "but Sawyer's going to help you."

"Yes, Master." I was so excited and wound up that I was shaking as Sawyer walked over to me slowly.

He cupped my face, gave me a tender kiss, then stepped back. Reaching for my shirt, he started taking charge. "Hands up."

It was different knowing Jackson was watching. Not in a bad way like Sawyer was afraid it would be, but it just made it more special. We were finally going to share it with our master. Sawyer might not be ready to be a pup with Master, but he was here with us and it was all that counted.

As Sawyer stripped my clothes off, Jackson pushed the coffee table to the side and sat down on the floor, watching closely. Everything about the way he was looking at us said he was taking it very seriously. Like he understood how much it meant to me. By the time Sawyer had me naked, I was still excited but not so frantic.

Jackson's heated gaze followed Sawyer's hands as they ran

over me soothingly. Sawyer finally gave me a kiss and spoke quietly. "All right, go kneel down in front of Master."

Everything was bouncing around inside my head, and all I wanted was for it to be quiet like it got when I played. Taking several slow breaths, I walked over to Jackson, trying to find my pup. He was so excited it was hard to catch him. I kept that thought to myself though, because I knew it wouldn't sound right.

Going down on all fours in front of Jackson, I waited while Sawyer moved everything closer and sat down beside us. "Why don't you start petting him, Master?"

Sawyer's hand moved to my head, and I sighed as it went over my hair and down my neck, along my spine. He made the long soothing stroke several times before I felt Jackson's hand join him. The combination of their touches made everything better.

Closing my eyes, I felt the stress fading away. I'd known it would be perfect, but Sawyer's anxiety had built until I could feel it pressing down on me as well. Sawyer's hands moved away, but Jackson's touch continued. It was sure and steady, the long strokes not quite impersonal, but not like a lover either.

It was perfect.

Sawyer's voice was quiet as he started to speak. Jackson kept up the soothing caress and made soft noises, probably the same kinds he made to biological dogs. I wasn't sure he realized he was doing it. "Cooper wears kneepads almost every time he's a pup, even if we're inside, because he runs around so much."

"Do you?" Jackson's voice was even and warm, and I knew it didn't matter to him either way. He was just trying to understand.

"Sometimes. It depends on how the scene will go, and what we're doing. Most of the time, I'm relaxed and cuddly, so it doesn't seem necessary." Sawyer's voice was hesitant, but I was so proud of him for explaining what he liked.

"That makes sense. As playful as you both make him out to be, I think they would be necessary or he'd end up bruised." Jackson's hands ran down my thighs and around my knees.

I couldn't decide if I wanted to bark or moan. I was in that half-in, half-out headspace, and everything felt incredible. It was a perfect combination of soothing and arousing. Sawyer's hands gripped my thighs and pulled at my leg. It was such a familiar command that I knew what he wanted without him having to say anything.

Lifting my leg to the side, I felt the straps of the kneepads go around my leg. I expected him to move me around or even to just shift to the other side, but that wasn't the plan. Sawyer's voice was getting stronger as he spoke again. "Here, you put this one on. As he gets deeper into his role, he doesn't really talk much, so asking him questions doesn't do any good. Just give clear commands like you would to a biological dog."

Jackson's words were low and while not really commands, it was clear I wasn't expected to answer. It was little things like, "There we go, my pretty pup," and "We're going to get you all fixed up so you can play."

When the kneepads were on, Sawyer showed him how to put on my mitts. I was starting to sink into the role, and the excitement was beginning to build. I was going to get to run around, and Jackson would throw the ball. Sawyer would give me cuddles and would rub me down more.

When Sawyer's hands caressed my ass, my entire body started to wiggle. Jackson hadn't been surprised by anything, and now he was going to see how cute I looked when I wagged my tail. It was a light brown color that had flecks of something like glitter in it, so it sparkled when it waved back and forth.

Jackson gave a low chuckle that made me scrunch my eyes up, and my cock jerked. It was clearly erect and reacted to Jackson like it always did, but I wasn't sure how he would take it now. That was the only issue to figure out.

Even if puppy time was completely nonsexual, it would still be incredible to be able to play with him and have fun. When I heard the sound of the lube opening, I dropped my arms to the floor and arched my ass up. Jackson gave another happy sound, and he ran his thumb around my hole, not quite trying to play with it but definitely teasing me.

"I have a pup that is very excited for his tail." Jackson's words seemed to be growing more heated, but I wasn't sure if I was just hearing it because that was what I wanted to be there.

Sawyer's fingers caressed around my clenched opening, and the coolness of the lube made me shiver. When his finger eased in, I made a low, needy whine, and Jackson's hands started rubbing along my back again like he was trying to settle me down. He was a natural at it.

I just knew he would be.

"His, um, hits his prostate just right when he wags it, and he wags it a lot so...yeah...he likes it." I couldn't tell if Sawyer was embarrassed or just nervous, but his voice sounded slightly pinched.

I heard Jackson shift and the soft sound of a kiss, and I had to smile. Jackson's voice was warm and loving as he spoke to Sawyer. "And does your tail rub you the same way?"

I could almost hear the blush in Sawyer's voice as he responded. "Um, I picked out a shallower plug that doesn't put as much pressure on mine. It will hit it sometimes, but it mostly feels good, but not *great* like Cooper's does."

"Ah. That makes sense. Biological dogs need different things depending on breed, so the same would hold true with pups like you two. Does that mean you have distinct collars and things as well?" Jackson's question was simple to him, but I knew it would make Sawyer nervous.

Sawyer eased in a second finger, distracting me enough that I almost missed his careful response. "We have basic collars right now that match, but we thought that our master would buy us new special ones someday."

"Giving a pup a collar like that would be very important. Wouldn't it?" Jackson's words were even, and he kept up the soothing strokes.

"Yes." Sawyer's fingers pulled out, and I felt the base of the plug press against me. It slid in easily, filling me just enough to be wonderful. It wasn't the same as having Jackson and Sawyer make love to me, but it was close.

And it had my tail.

When it was fully seated, I clenched down and wagged the tail back and forth. Jackson inhaled softly, then I felt the lightest touch circle around the plug. "Wag your tail, pup."

I wagged it again, and he made a low pleasured sound. "Have you both picked out names...?" There was the slightest pause while he seemed to realize the answer, "Or is that something like the collars, something a master would give you?"

Sawyer's face had probably given the answer away, and he didn't respond, but he must have done something nonverbal because I heard another kiss. Jackson gave my ass a squeeze, and I wagged my tail again for him. "My good pups are going to need names then."

He was incredible.

"All right, last piece, my excitable pup." Jackson's hand moved away from my ass, and I knew he was picking up the collar. "Sit up, pup."

Then almost to himself, he mumbled low. "We're going to have to work out some commands and practice with you. I think the structure would be good for you."

So excited I was going to explode, I lowered my ass to the floor and sat up, still on all fours. Opening my eyes, I looked at Jackson for the first time as a pup. He had the same warm, loving expression he always did when he looked at me, with the hint of laughter that was never far behind.

There were other emotions floating around as well, but they were harder to define.

Nothing that scared me or made me think he was uncomfortable. It was incredibly new to him, so I knew there would be some hesitation and even some fears. That was normal. But nothing said it was too much or that he needed space to figure it out, so I let the last few straggling fears from Sawyer fade away.

"Let's get your collar on, pretty boy." His hands came up and wrapped the collar around my neck. It didn't take long until it was on, and I was his pup. Everything was simpler, and I just wanted to play and show him how excited I was to be with him.

Giving him a little bark, I backed up and crouched down and stuck my bottom up, wagging my tail. Sawyer seemed to be trying to let him figure it out, because it took another bark and a quick look to the couch before Jackson connected the dots. "Oh, you want to play. Where's your ball?"

Again, the question didn't really seem to be one that I was supposed to answer. I got the feeling he would talk to biological dogs the same way, and it was so cute I had to show him how perfect he was. Bouncing up to him, I gave his a hand a lick and backed away, barking again.

Jackson laughed and finally found the ball on the couch. "You're going to have so much fun out in the arena."

Carefully rolling the ball across the room, he smiled as I raced after it. It was everything I'd ever wanted. Jackson was going to be a wonderful master and the perfect boyfriend. Letting the rest of the real world fade away, I scampered around the furniture to the sound of Jackson's warm laughter and encouraging words.

19

JACKSON

I t was the most...I didn't even have a word to describe it.

The entire world felt like it had tilted on its axis, but somehow that seemed to bring it all into view. How had I not known this existed? He was so...happy...free...it was something else entirely. Nothing was weighing him down. He wasn't worried about bills or about to-do lists or even what movie we were going to watch.

It was just pure, delightful enjoyment.

There were some of the same feelings that I associated with having a biological dog as I watched him. The same pleasure when they were happy and in watching them play, but it was so different because it was also Cooper.

My sweet, excited, lovable boy was also my sweet, excitable, lovable pup.

I'd been right. There was no way I could have known how it would feel unless I was actually seeing it. I still wasn't sure how to define the emotions rushing through me, but I knew right away it wasn't going to push me away.

As Cooper scampered up and dropped the ball in front of me, his little tail wagging and excitement flooding through him,

I knew nothing was going to chase me away. Tossing the ball, I turned and reached around Sawyer to pull him closer.

"You're too far away. Come here." Not giving him a choice, because we both knew he really didn't want one, I pulled him onto my lap.

He let out a laugh and curled into me. Sawyer looked over to where Cooper was scrambling after the ball, not really trying to catch it, and then smiled up at me. "It honestly doesn't bother you? Even a little?"

I shrugged. "I don't know how to explain it. He's so happy and so…even *more* Cooper like this than he usually is, if that makes any sense. He doesn't have a care in the world as long as that ball doesn't slide under the coffee table again."

He'd stubbornly refused to even try to use a human form of logic to get the ball. He'd barked until Sawyer had gone to get it out. The depth with which he sank into the role was confusing and fascinating. I knew I had a lot of research to do to understand it all, but nothing about it bothered me.

One eyebrow went up. "Even the huge hard-on he's sporting?"

Cooper came over and dropped the ball, barking excitedly. Sawyer had mentioned that it had been days since Cooper was a pup, partly because of their schedule and partly because of how excited he was to show me his pup. So I'd had fair warning that he would play for a while before he wore himself out.

Holding the ball tight, trying not to let Sawyer slip off my lap, I gave Cooper…well, my pup, a command in a deep voice. "Sit."

His butt went down.

So cute.

Speak seemed wrong, so I tried something else. "Bark."

And he barked so enthusiastically, I threw the ball for him. As he dashed off, I looked back down at Sawyer. "It's Cooper. He's always turned-on. He's my little Energizer Bunny."

Sawyer laughed, but the answer didn't seem to satisfy him.

Did I have a problem with it? I didn't think so. I'd kind of ignored it. To begin with, everything else was more overwhelming than the fact that naked Cooper had a hard-on. Naked Cooper always had a hard-on, so it wasn't a big shocker.

When he came bounding over again, ball gripped tightly in his mouth, he dropped it in Sawyer's lap and barked again. Picking up his toy, I held it up, deciding to try more commands. "Wag."

His tail went back and forth at lightning speed and a little whine escaped. He'd been hard for ages, his cock bouncing around as he ran and chased the ball. All the movement had to be playing havoc on his prostate as the plug rubbed up against him.

When he finally relaxed and barked, clearly encouraging me to throw the ball, I shook my head. "No, pup."

Showing him the ball, I slowly lowered it to the floor. "Lie down."

We went through several rounds of commands, and eventually had it where he'd crouch down with his ass high in the air when told to *present*. It was kinky as hell, but his cock was so hard he was dripping precum and even Sawyer was watching, holding his breath.

I just had to keep reminding myself that the websites all said that how we played was up to us. If it was sexual for us, that was fine. If it wasn't, that was fine too. There were no right or wrong answers. "Good boy."

Cooper relaxed down to the floor as I ran my fingers through his hair and down his back. I couldn't reach very much from where I was sitting, but he seemed content. "That's my good pup."

He gave a quiet bark and turned his head to lick my hand. It was such a familiar gesture that it didn't seem out of place. He was my pup, and pups licked. "Come here, pup."

Cooper moved around so he was closer to me, his side pressed against my leg. Much better. Sawyer reached out and started petting Cooper's head, enjoying the quiet moment before he wanted to bounce and play again. The training course, with some slight modifications, would be a good idea for him. More mental stimulation for a pup.

When he started to shift, and I knew it was only seconds before he began barking for the ball, I picked it up again. "Present."

His whole body shivered, and he gave a needy whine. I wasn't sure if he realized I was completely aware of how turned-on he was nor not, but it was time to stop ignoring the elephant in the room. Or the hard-on...however it should be worded.

"Wag." It quickly became apparent when we were practicing commands that something about this angle pressed the plug into his prostate beautifully. He'd wagged his tail and then tried to stop. "No. Wag."

I got another whine, needy and perfect. "Good boy. Wag."

Shivers raced through him as the tail swung back and forth, clearly pushing him closer and closer to the edge. He kept going, finally understanding that he wasn't going to be allowed to stop. When the sensation was too perfect, he'd start to hump the air, his cock desperate for attention, and then he'd lose the orgasm that had been ready to crash over him.

Then we'd start again.

Wag.

Race.

Hump.

Wag.

Race.

Hump.

He was so incredible to watch. When I knew he couldn't wait any longer, when the sounds coming from him were too needy and frantic, I had to give my pup what he needed. I didn't overthink it. I let deeper emotions take control. I wanted to please him. I wanted to give him everything that he was begging for.

It didn't really matter what it was.

Reaching out, I let my hand start caressing his back, loving how his entire body was begging for more. Shivers racing through him, and the way his muscles clenched and twitched told the story of how desperate he was better than any words could have.

"That's my pup." Dropping my voice low, I let my hand start running the length of his side. "My beautiful pup. That's right. Wag for me."

He gave a low bark and whined, but the tail kept swinging. When I finally let my hand move under his belly and along to his cock, his movements were jerky and almost panicked. He wasn't afraid. Chasing the pleasure was all he could think of, and the fear that he might not get it was probably barreling through him.

At least, that was what I thought was happening. But even if I'd misread the signs, Sawyer would have said something, and he was so quiet I wanted to poke him and make sure he was alive.

That wouldn't exactly match the mood I was going for, though.

"My good pup. Show me how you wag." Closing the last distance, I wrapped my fingers around his cock while the toy tormented his prostate with the plug. It was all he needed. One ragged bark and he exploded, his cock jerking in my hand, and his body clenched down so hard on the tail it wasn't even moving. Shaking, he was milking every drop of pleasure he could.

When it was over, he sagged down onto the floor. His head managed to land on Sawyer's leg, but that seemed to be more by accident than anything else. He was finally exhausted. My sweet pup who'd chased the ball endlessly and barked and played just lay there quietly.

When he managed to move, it was only to open one eye. I got a little bark and then he closed it again. I was slightly sticky and didn't want to smear it all over him, but I wanted to pet him. Sawyer finally understood the problem because he gave a low laugh and reached for the tissues on the side table. "Here you go."

Once I was fairly clean, I gave Sawyer a tender kiss on the lips and reached out to pet Cooper in long lazy strokes. They were both quiet and content, but for different reasons. My two boys couldn't have been more different, but they were perfect together and perfect for me. I just hoped they saw that as clearly as I did.

Kissing Sawyer's forehead, I pulled him even closer. "Thank you for taking the chance and emailing me. I can see how hard that was for you now."

I could feel his smile and he nodded slowly. "Thank you for taking the chance on us and looking past what must have been a shocking letter."

He was right, but something about it had pulled to me from the moment I looked at it. "I knew you were special the first time I ever read that email. I just never pictured how quickly everything would change."

"Too fast?" He didn't seem concerned, just curious.

"No. Surprisingly not. It feels like I've known you both for much longer than just what the calendar says."

"Sometimes you just know. I went up to Cooper the first time I met him. Some bullies were going to use him for target practice, and I just couldn't walk away. I knew we'd be friends, but I never imagined how it would all work out."

"Things don't always end up how you pictured them, but in

this case, I think it's better than anything I could have dreamed up."

"You never pictured having two pups?" Laughter came through in his voice, but he snuggled close.

"Not as special as you two." I kissed his forehead again. "No one could be as special as my two pups."

Finding them might have been an accident, but I was their master by choice, and I knew there was nowhere else I'd rather be. And as I held my two men, my boys, my pups, I knew someday, Sawyer would understand it as well.

But we had the time; I wasn't going anywhere.

ABOUT M.A. INNES

M.A. Innes is the pseudonym for best-selling author Shaw Montgomery. While Shaw writes femdom and m/m erotic romance. M.A. Innes is the side of Shaw that wants to write about topics that are more taboo. If you liked the book, please leave a short review. It is greatly appreciated.

Do you want to join the newsletter? Help with character names and get free sneak peeks at what's coming up? Just click on the link.

https://www.subscribepage.com/n1i5u1

You can also get information on upcoming books and ideas on Shaw's website.

www.authorshawmontgomery.com

ALSO BY M.A. INNES

AVAILABLE ON AUDIOBOOK

Secrets In The Dark
   Flawed Perfection
   Silent Strength
   Quiet Strength (Coming Spring 2018)

ALSO BY SHAW MONTGOMERY

AVAILABLE ON AUDIOBOOK

Bound & Controlled Book 1: Garrett's story
Bound & Controlled Book 2: Brent's story
Bound & Controlled Book 3: Grant's story (Coming March 2018)
Bound & Controlled Book 4: Bryce's story (Coming April 2018)
Bound & Controlled: The Complete Series (Coming May 2018)

"Alright. We're going to get the hard stuff out of the way first. If you're still interested afterward, I'll show you around. Because it's a good-size apartment, and I'm not asking an arm and a leg for the rent." I hadn't even given the guy a chance to say anything as I opened the door. I'd just charged right in, doing my best to ignore his big brown eyes and startled expression.

Reminding myself that I did *not* need to get distracted by the sexy teddy bear of a guy before I even knew how crazy he was, I kept going. "I work from home, so I'm here nearly all the time. I'm a little OCD, so if you're messy, that's going to be a problem. I'm gay. So if you're a homophobe, or something crazy like those morons with the signs, I don't even want to hear it. I've gotten the insanity from a dozen different people over the past week, so keep that shit to yourself." He hadn't run screaming like the uptight accountant, or crying like the short guy who'd started losing it because evidently, *all the good apartments were gay*, so it was a good sign.

Too bad I wasn't done with the speech. "And there's a washer and dryer in the unit, so that means you don't have to schlep things down to the laundromat, but that also means we're going to see each other's clothes. Well, I wear women's underwear, and I don't plan on panicking every time I do my goddamned laundry. If that's a problem, you already know the way out of the building."

His mouth was open, but nothing came out. Had I broken him already? It'd taken six months before the last one lost it. "Hello? You still interested?"

He finally blinked, long eyelashes drawing even more attention to his sexy brown eyes. "You weren't asking for a security deposit. Just the first month's rent?"

Not what I was expecting him to say, but okay. "Yup."

"Then I'd like to see it, please." His voice came out slightly stiff but even.

Looked like I might have found a keeper.

Well, roommate anyway. Finding anything beyond that would just be ridiculous, considering how hard it was to find a decent roommate. If I couldn't find a reasonable stranger to ignore what I liked, how could I expect to find a date who would?

"Come on in, and I'll show you around." I stepped back from the door, trying to seem a little friendlier. If he wasn't scared off by everything else, I didn't want to make him think I was an ogre. I was usually pretty reasonable as long as I didn't have to deal with day after day of morons and idiots.

There was a reason I worked from home and not with the average customer.

The new guy was a short little thing but broad enough that his frame hinted at muscles under his clothes. Not that I was looking. Statistically, he was probably straight, but with the increasing number of people who defined their sexuality on less rigid terms, there were reasonable odds he was at least curious.

Not that it mattered.

"The living room is this way." The condo actually had a lot

of space for a place so close to downtown. The location and size were just some of the reasons I'd grabbed it up. But they were also the reasons I usually had a roommate.

I was financially sound enough in my career that I didn't need to have someone else to split the mortgage and utilities with, but it made my budget a lot easier. I didn't have a lot of crazy expenses, but I liked to travel, and having someone around to watch the apartment as well as let me save more worked out perfectly. And with my goal of paying off the mortgage early, it meant I didn't have to compromise.

Usually.

I hadn't been so lucky lately.

When I'd first started looking for roommates, I'd ended up with women, and that'd worked out fairly well. Until the last one turned out to be a bit off and didn't believe I was actually gay. After she'd only been living in the condo a month, I'd found her naked in my bed.

After that, everything had gone downhill. Fast.

I'd finally managed to get her out, but it'd been an awkward couple of months. When I'd started looking for another roommate, I'd ended up with a straight guy who couldn't manage to understand that every look wasn't a come-on. I'd never been more grateful when he'd gotten transferred to the Midwest somewhere.

The next one only lasted two days until he found my panties in the laundry. So I wasn't even sure I could claim him as a roommate. Whoever the hell the new guy was, at least he didn't seem to be easily fazed.

He simply walked around the living room, calm and curious. "Will I have enough space in the kitchen? My last roommate had issues with giving me a reasonable amount of room. I don't mind sharing, but one small shelf in the fridge and one in the pantry isn't enough to cook anything."

"I don't mind making as much space as you need. I don't

have a lot of kitchen gadgets, so there's plenty of empty shelves. I also don't mind you borrowing stuff as long as you replace it and clean up after yourself." I gave him a careless shrug and pointed toward the kitchen. "Take a look."

He nodded and headed toward the archway that separated the two rooms. Looking back at me, he paused and stretched out his hand. "I'm Reece, nice to meet you."

"Houston. Same." I wasn't going to get overly friendly until I knew he was actually staying—and sane.

I waited at the door while Reece walked into the kitchen, opening cabinets and going through it in more detail than anyone else I'd ever had living there. Could he actually cook? I wasn't bad, but when it was just me, I didn't always see the point.

I tried to look at the space through his eyes. I remembered the real estate agent talking about the amount of counter space and the upgraded appliances, but I'd tuned it out after making sure it was on par with everything else in the neighborhood.

Kitchens and bathrooms helped with resale value, but beyond that, I didn't really notice them. Granite counters, well-made cabinets, and a good layout meant I wasn't going to have to replace much if I decided to sell sooner than I'd planned.

Finally nodding, like it'd gotten his seal of approval, Reece glanced over at me. "Can I see the bedroom?"

"Sure." I started heading for the back of the condo while he followed. "You have the first bedroom and the hall bath. It's a decent size, but if you need another space for an office or something, let me know, and we might be able to work something out."

He glanced in the bathroom, nodding quietly again, then crossed the hall to go in the bedroom. The master and guest bedrooms were both fairly large. There was one small room, but I used that for an office. So I wasn't surprised when he made a pleased sound and smiled.

"I've seen a few lately that were like large closets and that's it." He started wandering around the empty room and seemed to be mentally mapping it out, pacing steps and walking in odd patterns. "I've never lived in a place where people were so proud of tiny apartments."

"Have you lived here long?"

"No. I just took a new job. I'm living in temporary corporate housing now, but I want my own space." He kept wandering around the room, looking in the closet and pacing more steps off. "I think this will work."

He gave me a long look, those big brown eyes staring me. He was going to have to stop doing that to me. "Any other rules or facts I should be aware of? I'm not a big partier, but I'd like to be able to bring someone home eventually without it causing problems."

I shrugged. I didn't care who he fucked as long as they didn't drive me nuts. "Just keep the noise level down and don't get naked in the communal spaces, then we'll be good."

His face scrunched up, and his head tilted like he didn't understand what I meant, so I felt the need to explain. "I've had some interesting roommates in the last year."

Reece nodded slowly. "I can promise I'll keep my clothes on, things fairly clean, and no loud parties."

"Works for me. I have a contract in the kitchen and a few basic questions about your income. I'll let you read through it and make sure you don't have any issues with it." As we headed back to the other side of the condo, Reece started to talk more.

"The ad I read said moving in right away is fine?" His voice was calm as he studied the space while we walked through. He seemed nothing like the last applicants and nothing like my previous roommates; I could only hope that would be a good thing.

"Sure." I was saving up for another trip to Europe, so sooner was better than later.

"Good. I talked to the people who are storing my moving POD, and they said getting me worked in wouldn't be a problem if I found something quickly." As he wandered into the kitchen, he looked around again. "You have a great kitchen. You're sure my using it or putting stuff in the cabinets isn't going to be a problem? My last roommate said he'd clear out space for me, but it wasn't enough to unpack even one box, so I had to eat out almost constantly."

I gestured around the room as I walked over to pull out the paperwork from the folder. "No, if it's empty, go for it. I eat out a lot, so it's not going to bother me unless you end up leaving it a mess."

He glanced up at me, and it had to be the short hair making his eyes so noticeable. "Well, I usually end up making too much, so if there are leftovers, feel free to help yourself."

"Thanks." I'd learned the hard way not to believe that. I wasn't going to argue with him, though. "Here you go."

Taking the papers, he started reading through them. It was a standard rental contract, so I didn't think he'd find anything odd. After going through a few points, discussing his finances, and writing in the starting and ending date of the lease, we signed, and it was done.

I was relieved to have it over, because finding someone had taken a ridiculous amount of time. But the tension wasn't going to leave until I figured out his form of crazy. The calm, teddy bear expression was only going to last so long.

He'd said he wasn't a big partier, but that probably meant he liked to get stoned on his own. Having someone over probably meant he had a revolving door of women in his bedroom. More than likely, I was going to have to listen to some girl scream out how incredible he was every night.

God, that had been a long three months.

I wasn't sure I could go back to getting that little sleep

again. The sleepy pot smoker was starting to sound better and better. "So, you said you're in IT?"

That had to mean drug screenings, right?

Reece leaned back in the chair, and his shirt stretched across his chest, clearly outlining the muscles under his clothes. I tried not to stare, but unlike the paranoid skinny straight guy who had to have been a closet case, Reece was actually my type.

Shit.

I loved short, stocky guys. Sexy men that could be manhandled without the risk of actually hurting them got me going. I was going to have to be careful. No matter how hot he was, making the guy uncomfortable wasn't something that I wanted to do.

Reece nodded. "Yes, I generally work with smaller companies that are in the process of growing and are starting to need their own IT department. My new job is with an internet startup that's finally expanded past what their current staff can handle and needs actual IT help. After their site crashed a few times last month because of the amount of traffic, they realized what they had wasn't working."

"Sounds interesting." Not really, but it was better than the tax guy. And I was in finance, so that was saying something.

Reece's smile went from pleasant to filled with real pleasure. It was distracting as hell. Maybe I could convince him to wear a mask around the condo. But that image was too distracting, so I pushed it away and tried to listen. "It's a great opportunity. I'm getting in on the ground floor with them, and I'm going to be in charge of the whole department."

Then he gave a laugh and shrugged carelessly. "Which only consists of me right now, and a few tech-savvy people in their marketing department, at least some of the time, but they've talked about expanding it over the next couple of years. I think it's going to be a good fit."

"That's great. Getting in while a company is still growing

can be wonderful in the long run." Not sure what else to say that wouldn't turn into a business lecture, I pushed back from the table. "Let me get you a key. When do you think your stuff will get here?"

"Thanks. Two or three days tops, at least according to the manager I talked to yesterday. He said they had a light week, and that if I could find something quickly, I wouldn't have to wait long to get it delivered." Reece followed me out to the living room. "I'll give you a call as soon as I know what the exact timeline looks like. I'm aiming for Friday afternoon, if they can make that work. It's a tight turnaround for them, but it would give me the whole weekend to get settled."

"That's probably best." Digging around in the side table drawer, I found one of the extra keys. "You probably have a lot to get straightened out at the new job."

Handing it over, I tried not to notice the way his eyes lit up again as he talked about his work. "Actually, the couple of guys who were doing it before had a good handle on it. There's just no way they can keep doing two jobs. The pay's pretty good for a smaller company, and everyone seems friendly. I think it's going to be interesting."

After showing him a few more things around the apartment and helping him take some measurements of the room, he was on his way with a promise to call me with the exact time for the movers.

Two days wasn't a lot of time for them to arrange delivery, but he seemed confident. So I made myself a mental reminder to check my schedule and make sure I didn't have any meetings planned that day.

I probably should've gotten to know him more or offered to take the guy out to lunch, but I just wanted to enjoy my last moments of quiet before the storm hit. He seemed nice, but so had the rest of them at first.

As I closed the door, I started mentally rearranging my

finances to see how it would work if I decided not to get another roommate. It would be doable if I cut back on my monthly savings and investment goals and stretched out the time between vacations.

But growing the business was probably a better solution.

I'd worked countless hours through my twenties, burning the candle at both ends, building up my own personal savings and investment portfolio and planning out the best way to work on my own. As much as I loved the stock market, talking to countless people who never listened and answering simple questions over and over wasn't what I was suited for.

I just didn't have the patience for it.

However, day trading my own investments and setting up business proposals for new companies was something I was comfortable with. If I took on a few more new clients over the next couple of months, it would give me the flexibility I needed, just in case Reese turned out to be nuts as well.

Looking at the time on my phone, I started heading back to the bedroom. My brain was in too many places at once to settle down to work. I'd done as much as I could on my own trading before Reece had arrived, and I wasn't set to start on the next business plan for about a week, so it wasn't a bad day to play hooky. The gym was probably the best bet.

I started stripping off my clothes as I entered the bedroom, taking a moment to close the door. I was going to have to start paying attention to things like that again. Tossing my shirt on the bed, my shoes went next, and I continued on to everything else.

Keeping a strict schedule and dressing for work, even though it was more business casual than Wall Street, made working from home easier. But as I grabbed workout gear and headed into the bathroom in just my underwear, I had to laugh.

Looking in the mirror, I shook my head. How was I the sanest person out of all the roommates I'd had lately? The businessman Dom in the bright pink boy short panties should *not* have been the first choice for most normal. Not that I was worried about what "normal" was, but still, it was getting ridiculous.

"You need to go to the gym more. Those panties looked much better five pounds ago." I shook my finger at the man in the mirror. But for someone who sat most of the day, and who had too easy access to the fridge, I wasn't looking too bad.

I couldn't help but try to picture what Reece would think.

I'd long ago accepted what I liked and who I was, but I couldn't help guessing at his reaction. He'd been calm and unfazed when I'd blurted it out, but how would the rest hit him? Doms were supposed to be tough and dressed in all leather, swinging a paddle or a crop, not decked out in satin panties or a lace bodysuit.

I looked damned good in that bodysuit, extra five pounds or not.

"Okay, off to the gym, lazy. You'll never get that six-pack back looking at yourself in the mirror or thinking about your new roommate." Of the two, finding the energy to exercise would probably be harder. All I had to do was wait until Reece moved in, and then the shine would fade. There was no way he'd be as perfect as my imagination wanted to make him.

A man who was strong, compact, sexy, not shocked by the whole feminine underwear thing, gay, and submissive wasn't someone that was just going to show up randomly on my doorstep.

Made in the USA
Monee, IL
22 June 2024

60348108R00135